Rocky Basin

Book Twenty in the Redemption Mountain Historical Western Romance Series

SHIRLEEN DAVIES

Books Series by Shirleen Davies

Historical Western Romances

Redemption Mountain
MacLarens of Fire Mountain Historical
MacLarens of Boundary Mountain

Romantic Suspense

Eternal Brethren Military Romantic Suspense
Peregrine Bay Romantic Suspense

Contemporary Western Romance

MacLarens of Fire Mountain Contemporary
Macklins of Whiskey Bend

The best way to stay in touch is to subscribe to my newsletter. Go to my Website *www.shirleendavies.com* and fill in your email and name in the Join My Newsletter boxes. That's it!

I care about quality, so if you find something in error,
please contact me via email at
shirleen@shirleendavies.com

Description

Will her love be enough to help this former gunslinger recapture what's left of his heart...and his soul?

Griffin MacKenzie loves the town of Splendor, Montana, its people, and his work as a lawyer. His days of traveling the west as a gun for hire are far behind him, and for the first time, he feels settled. Except for an attraction to a beautiful young woman he can't rid from his thoughts.

Carrie Galloway longs for more than her work as a nurse. As much as she craves a family, Carrie has no desire to marry for the sake of companionship and children. Her heart desires love—the deep, abiding kind she witnesses in other Splendor couples.

A growing friendship between Griff and Carrie opens the possibility of more, until his past catches up to him. An old enemy appears, threatening their lives, as well as a shared future.

Will Griff allow his past to destroy a future with the woman he's come to love? Or will he fight for a life he increasingly wants to claim?

Rocky Basin is book twenty in the Redemption Mountain historical western romance series by bestseller Shirleen Davies. It is a full-length novel with and no cliffhanger and a guaranteed HEA.

Rocky Basin

Chapter One

Splendor Montana
Winter 1873

Griffin MacKenzie pulled the collar of his thick wool coat up before shoving his hat lower on his forehead. The snow whipped around him, slowing his pace, forcing him to seek shelter in the closest establishment.

Even at three in the afternoon, the tinny piano in Finn's Saloon pounded through the batwing doors. Brushing snow from his coat, Griff took a quick look around, his gaze passing over a table of cowboys playing cards. A glint of recognition hit.

He whipped his gaze toward a familiar face in time to see the man stand, draw his six-shooter, and fire directly at him. A whoosh of air passed within an inch of one ear.

Old habits took over. Dropping to one knee, Griff shoved his coat aside, sliding his gun from the holster. To onlookers, it appeared he didn't aim before firing. They were wrong.

Experience kicked in, his innate ability to aim and shoot simultaneously saving his life today, the same as in the past. His bullet hit true, blowing a hole in the man's chest. Stunned eyes met Griff's an instant before the gunman toppled backward, taking a chair to the floor with him.

Before he could stand, another man drew a six-shooter and fired, missing Griff by a good two feet. A third slid from his chair to the floor. His shot also missed. Griff pulled the trigger three times, wounding both men, their guns crashing to the floor.

Rising, Griff didn't seem to notice the total quiet in a room bursting with activity a minute earlier. Without holstering his gun, he walked past the two wounded men, stopping where the original shooter sprawled, arms flung to his sides, legs askew. His mouth twisted into a permanent grimace, eyes wide and vacant.

Griff hadn't been wrong. Morty Gallant had found him.

Stiffening as the hairs on the back of his neck prickled, he turned to face a fourth man aiming a six-shooter at his head. A slow grin crossed Griff's face.

"You got nothing to smile about, MacKenzie."

"Shows how much you know, Purdy."

The man opened his mouth to respond, clamping it shut when the cold metal of a muzzle dug into the back of his head.

"Drop it and turn around." Dutch McFarlin's hard, unwavering voice rang through the still air. "Now." The deputy always showed enormous patience, until he didn't.

Purdy flashed Griff a smirk before dropping his gun. Keeping his arms raised, he turned to stare into resolute blue eyes, taking an involuntary step away. At over six feet tall, with wavy, dark red hair and broad, muscled chest, Dutch was a formidable figure.

Pulling handcuffs from a pocket, he tossed them at Griff. "You mind?" He looked at the bartender. "Get the undertaker."

"Not at all." Locking the metal cuffs, he twisted them enough to get a growled curse from Purdy. One side of his mouth lifted in a grin. "He's all yours, Dutch."

"You're not done yet. I need to write down your statement. Or you can tell it to Gabe if he's at the jail."

Even though the extra time delayed his plans for the afternoon, he gave a curt nod, holding the doors wide for Dutch and Purdy to exit. The storm had cleared enough to see up and down Frontier Street. Except for a wagon loaded with supplies from the general store, and a trio of riders, the road was empty.

Dutch waved at two of the newest deputies walking toward them. Jonas Taylor and Tucker Nolan had been hired, along with Morgan Wheeler, a few months earlier.

"There are two wounded men in Finn's. Take them to the jail, then get one of the doctors."

Jonas flashed him a grin. "We'll get them, Dutch."

Crossing to the jail, Griff threw the door open, stepping aside to let Dutch and Purdy enter. Sheriff Gabe Evans stood at the stove, stirring sugar into his cup of coffee. Taking a sip, he showed no real concern.

"Who do you have, Dutch?"

"Purdy Dwyer," Griff answered for the deputy. "He meant to shoot me."

Shoving the prisoner's back, Dutch led him to the cells. "There's a body at Finn's. The bartender's sending for the undertaker."

The door slammed open, Jonas and Tucker escorting two men inside. One limped from a wound to his thigh while the other gripped his blood-soaked shirt. Without a word, they joined Dutch in the back, locking them in separate cells.

Lifting a brow at Griff, Gabe filled two more cups, setting all three on the desk. "A body?"

"Morty Gallant shot at me. My bullet was true. There were at least a dozen witnesses." Grabbing a cup, Griff took a swallow. "Best coffee in Splendor."

"It ought to be. I have it delivered from my hotels in New York. Tell me about Gallant and Dwyer."

Features clouding, Griff scrubbed a hand down his face. He hated revisiting his time as a paid gunman and Range Detective. The first was considered no better than a hired killer. The second an enforcer of the law. In his experience, one was no different than the other.

"You know I was a Range Detective."

Gabe nodded, pointing to the third cup of coffee when Dutch joined them. Jonas and Tucker poured their own, taking the last two chairs.

"Their gang was active in Texas, hitting a different ranch every week, stealing as many as a hundred head at a time. Most times, twenty-five or less. I had a hunch they'd go after a specific rancher who planned on moving a small herd to another pasture. He'd already been hit once, but it had been a while. I made sure word about the move got out through the ranch hands. Sure enough, Morty, Purdy, and their men swept in at night. We were ready. Eight of the gang's men were killed, including Morty's nephew. Dwyer, Gallant, and the rest of their men got away. I clipped Morty in the arm, but it didn't slow him down. Word was they ended up in Oklahoma, then Nebraska."

"Now they're after you," Gabe said.

Griff shook his head. "Doesn't make sense. Morty looked surprised to see me."

Dutch snorted a chuckle. "He sure reacted quickly for not expecting you."

"And if he hadn't come to Splendor for you, it's odd Gallant recognized you after so many years," Gabe added.

Rubbing his chin, Griff's mind went back to that day on the edges of an enormous Texas ranch. He'd been on the job for weeks with little progress. Perhaps frustration guided his actions.

The sight of so many dead young men still haunted him. Eight had died, Griff doing most of the killing. Instead of gratitude for ending the rustling, he received distrustful stares and suspicion. Those on the ranch, and townsfolk, were ready for him to leave. A chair scraping against the rough wood planks brought him back to the present.

"Unless there's something more you need, I should get going." Standing, he stepped outside into a darkening sky.

The storm increased while Griff had been in the jail. Snow covered the boardwalk and streets, the number of people slowing to a few brave souls.

His pocket watch showed three in the afternoon. The bank would now be closed, and the saloons open. Cowboys in Finn's would've returned to their card playing within minutes of the shooting. Nothing much surprised anyone in the expanding frontier town.

Walking to Chinatown, he turned onto Grant Street. All the Chinese businesses were crammed into the buildings on both sides. The interiors were small, about half the size of shops on Frontier or Palace Street. The shops were varied.

Griff passed the Chinese newspaper, bookstore, a shop featuring traditional clothing and silk fabric, tailor shop, grocery, restaurants, and laundry on his way to his destination. A theater offering Chinese plays had been built in the last year. Next to it was a temple they called Joss House. On the other side of the temple was a gift and curio shop. Griff knew a gambling den was hidden in the back, the same as he knew an opium den took up space behind the laundry.

He didn't linger at any of the businesses on his way to his destination. Chin Jun, the unofficial mayor of Chinatown, owned an herb and tea shop. The shelves were filled with interesting potions and teas. The latter was the real reason for his visits.

The cramped layout and narrow aisles made it difficult for a man of Griff's size to locate specific products. He knew not to try.

Chin Jun emerged from the back, listening to the young man following him who spoke in rapid Chinese. Seeing Griff, he held up a hand, silencing the conversation. Making a slight bow, he rushed toward him.

"It is good to see you, Griffin MacKenzie."

"Chin Jun. You appear well."

Cackling, the older man swept his hand around the tight space. "I use my herbs. You stay. I will get the tea."

Hands clasped in front of him, the younger man stared at Griff. "You are a friend of my father's?"

Surprised at the perfect English, he nodded. "I am. Do you work in the shop?"

An odd expression crossed his face before giving a brisk shake of his head. "I'll be going to school in San Francisco. I want to be a lawyer."

"To help the people in Chinatown?"

"Them and others."

Griff searched in a pocket, retrieving a card. *Griffin MacKenzie, Attorney-at-Law.* "Come see me when you've finished your studies. What's your name?"

The young man stared at the card, licked his lips, then met Griff's interested gaze. "I am Chin Jinping, the oldest son."

His father walked toward them, holding a fabric pouch out to Griff. "You pay now?"

Pulling coins from a pocket, he held them out. "Thank you, Chin Jun. I'll be back next week." He turned toward Chin Jinping. "Good luck with your studies."

Stepping into the building storm, he stuffed the pouch into a pocket. Griff suspected the tea he drank to ease the pain in one leg included more than herbs. A pinch of morphine was his guess, although he never asked. If overused, the brew could become an unbreakable habit, as it did with soldiers losing limbs during the war.

Rushing back in the direction he'd come, he turned onto Worthington Street. Ahead was the small house used by Morgan, Tucker, and Jonas. They'd been deputies in St. Louis, then Texas Rangers before riding north to Big Pine. Sheriff Parker Sterling didn't have a need for all three. Instead, he sent them to Gabe in Splendor.

Griff stopped, grimacing at the recurring pain in his left hip and knee. Leaning his shoulder against the back wall of Ruby's Grand Palace, he absently rubbed both. The pain always grew worse in the cold. It hadn't bothered him much in Conviction, California.

For a brief moment, he wondered why he'd insisted on traveling with Bram and Thane MacLaren to the freezing winters of Montana. Glancing at the clinic in front of him, he shoved aside the thought.

He had plans for the future, and the woman inside played a starring role.

Chapter Two

Carrie Galloway stifled a grin at the way Curly Post squirmed. The grizzled cowhand worked for Dom Lucero, doing whatever was needed to keep the ranch running.

He'd been pulling a stray from the thorny bush holding the young animal hostage. Cutting the long vines, paying no attention to the cow behind him, Curly didn't anticipate the mother slamming into him. The force sent him into the center of the bush, slicing a six-inch slice in his thigh. Carrie estimated it to be half an inch deep. She didn't know what threat Dom used to get Curly into a wagon, but it worked.

Dom leaned against the frame, his arms crossed. His expression conveyed his annoyance with Curly. It had no effect on the older man, who smirked at his boss. Any other ranch hand would've heeded the warning in Dom's eyes. Not Curly.

"You have a beau, little lady?"

Carrie's eyes crinkled at the corners, a choked laugh escaping. "No, Mr. Post, I don't."

"Leave Miss Galloway alone, Curly." Dom's gaze moved to Carrie. "He can be a pain in my butt on his best days."

"I ain't no pain in anything, boss."

"It's all right, Dom. Mr. Post is entertaining." She wiped away the blood as she sutured the wound.

"See there, boss. I'm entertaining."

"Yeah, a real joker."

Carrie dabbed again at the wound as she finished one more suture. "Five minutes and I'll be done."

"You want to have supper with me tonight, missy?"

Dom blew out a frustrated breath. "Stop right there, Curly. Miss Galloway does not want to have supper with you."

Curly lifted a narrowed gaze from his thigh. "She might. Right, missy?"

"Mr. Post, you are the brightest spot in my regular routine. Still, I'd have to decline your generous offer." Wiping the wound one last time, she straightened, tossing the cloth into a bucket. "We have laudanum for the pain."

"Don't need nothing." Sliding to the floor, Curly gripped the edge of the bed, his legs buckling. Dom moved to his side, sliding an arm around him.

"Take it easy, old man."

"I ain't old." One hand tightened on the bed as he leaned into Dom. "We got whiskey in the wagon?"

Carrie opened a cupboard, clutching a bottle. Removing the cork, she put it to Curly's lips. "Drink some of this, Mr. Post."

Doing as she said, he gulped several swallows before lifting his head, attempting a smile. "Whiskey's a darned sight better than laudanum."

"That's what I've been told." Tapping the cork back in place, she set it aside. Moving to Curly's other side, she slipped an arm behind him, nodding at Dom.

A man passing by the clinic helped them load Curly into the back of the wagon. She waved when Dom slapped the lines and moved on.

Standing outside longer than necessary, she watched shadows play on the buildings as the sun began its descent behind the western mountains. Her attention moved down the street, landing on the small house she shared with fellow nurse, Georgina Wise.

Lately, Georgina had been considering the idea of leaving Splendor, traveling to San Francisco. She hoped Carrie would go with her.

Watching soft flakes of snow drift down to form a blanket of white, Carrie felt herself shiver. The cold of Montana wasn't the same as in New York. She found it easier to be outside as the temperature dropped. And the summers? Carrie loved the wildflowers, green of the meadows, and deep blue of the sky.

Thinking about her time in Splendor, she came to an easy decision. She wouldn't be traveling west with Georgina.

"Carrie?" Glancing over her shoulder at the sound of Doctor Clay McCord's voice, she took one last glance up and down the street before stepping into the clinic.

Georgina served up two bowls of stew, setting both on the table as Carrie emerged from her bedroom. They took turns fixing supper and cleaning dishes depending on their work schedule at the clinic.

"Smells wonderful, Georgie." Carrie didn't meet Georgina's eyes, afraid her friend would sense the lie. Not the best cook, there were times Carrie choked down the food with the help of copious amounts of coffee or tea.

"I added more salt this time. Suzanne at the boardinghouse suggested some other herbs, so I tried a couple of those."

"I'm sure it will be as good as all your other meals." Carrie congratulated herself for keeping a straight face.

What the town called the mail order brides, the two had arrived in Splendor with three other women more than two years earlier. All were from New York, and were friends of Rachel Pelletier. Her husband, Dax, and his brother, Luke, were the owners of the largest ranch in western Montana. Of the five, only attorney Francesca O'Reilly Boudreaux had married.

Unlike Georgina, Carrie wasn't in a hurry to give up her short period of independence. As the oldest of six, she found herself being the mother hers couldn't be. As always, her heart squeezed every time her thoughts went to the woman who'd died too soon, leaving a grieving husband and a houseful of children.

Working three jobs, her father had succumbed to a failing heart while Carrie trained as a nurse. She and her oldest brother, Samuel, were left to take care of themselves, while the four youngest were sent to relatives.

Samuel found work as a dock worker by day, and bartender at a nearby tavern at night, allowing Carrie to finish her studies. She'd found work at a clinic, which is where she met Rachel. They'd become fast friends.

Taking a small bite of stew, Carrie almost choked on the overabundance of salt. Careful not to tip over her cup, she swallowed several gulps of coffee, almost burning her mouth.

"What do you think?"

Ignoring the way her eyes watered, Carrie scooped up another small bite. "Getting better each time, Georgie." She was glad for the lie when her friend's mouth tipped up in a small smile.

"Have you thought about San Francisco?"

Carrie knew the question would be coming, had hoped it wouldn't be so soon. "I'm still considering it."

"I know you love Splendor, but aren't you curious about seeing the Pacific Ocean and California?"

"Not as curious as you, Georgie."

Biting into a larger than usual crystal of salt, she turned her head away, unable to stifle a wince. Picking up her cup, she sighed, realizing it was empty. Trying not to rush, she stepped to the stove, filling it with the last of the coffee.

"I can make more." Georgina set down her napkin, preparing to stand.

"I'll do it." Carrie wondered how long it would take before Georgina mentioned the trip again. Except for a certain ranch hand her friend was attracted to, there'd been little else they discussed since she first considered leaving Splendor.

"I'm thinking about leaving the end of March."

Turning away from the stove, Carrie made a mental calculation. "That's less than six weeks. Wouldn't it be best to stay until the end of April? I understand the stagecoach has a better chance of not being snowbound the longer you wait."

"Bernie Griggs advised me not to leave before the first of April." Georgina mentioned the clerk at the stage and Western Union office. "You could be right, though. Staying a few weeks more won't make much difference."

Carrie clasped her hands in front of her, waiting for the coffee to finish. "The doctors will appreciate the added time to find a replacement. Assuming they can find someone."

Both women knew how hard it was to find trained nurses in this remote area of Montana. Even though they lived at the Pelletier ranch, Rachel and Rosemary Masters had worked long after their marriages. Carrie suspected it was one reason Rachel invited her and Georgina to travel west.

Carrying the pot to the table, Carrie filled Georgina's cup, then her own. Returning the coffeepot to the stove, she whirled around at a sharp rap on their door.

"I wonder who that could be?" Standing, Georgina closed the short distance to the door. Opening it, the corners of her mouth lifted, her gaze landing on a package in his hand. "Mr. MacKenzie. What a pleasant surprise."

"Miss Wise." He looked past her to see Carrie staring at him. "Miss Galloway."

Carrie saw the snow on his clothes. "Mr. MacKenzie. Won't you come in?"

Removing his hat, he tapped it against his leg before brushing snow from his coat, and stepping inside. A smile, directed at Carrie, had her stomach clenching. She'd always found him handsome, but always believed she'd been invisible to him.

Her good friend, Francesca, was his partner in the law practice. She spoke of him in glowing terms, saying often how lucky she'd been to have him ride all the way from California to take the position.

"Would you, um...like some coffee?"

"If it isn't too much trouble." Setting his hat on a hook, he did the same with his coat.

Coming up beside him, Georgina nodded toward the package in his hand. "What do you have there?"

Carrie bit her lip at her friend's bold question. If a thought popped into Georgina's head, it came out her mouth.

"I had supper at the Eagle's Nest with Gabe and Lena Evans. May Covington brought out a package for me and them." Placing it on the table, he removed the wrapping to reveal several slices of lemon pie. "I hoped you two would share it with me."

"Oh, my." Georgina rushed to open a cupboard, pulling down three plates before lifting forks from a drawer.

Setting a third cup of coffee on the table, Carrie motioned toward a chair. "It was quite thoughtful of you to think of us, Mr. MacKenzie."

Instead of sitting, he pulled out her chair, then one for Georgina before taking his own seat. "I prefer sharing instead of hoarding my bounty."

Not waiting, Georgina slid a piece of pie onto each plate, handing one to Carrie, another to Griffin. Taking a bite, she hummed in pleasure.

Carrie continued to watch him under lowered lashes. Other than attending a few weddings, she'd never been this close to him, or noticed his raw masculinity. He'd always been Francesca's business partner, a man with a quick mind and easy smile.

Tonight, he seemed much more. Deeper. More complex. A man worth getting to know.

Chapter Three

The clinic was packed with people when Carrie arrived a little before eight the next morning. Mothers with sick children, a local merchant pressing a cloth to a gash in his leg, and two of Ruby Walsh's girls from the Palace, one bent over at the waist.

"We'll get to each of you as soon as possible." Hearing a scream from an examination room, she rushed forward, opening the door a crack.

Inside, Hawke DeBell held his wife's hand, his panicked gaze meeting Carrie's. Beauty's face was twisted in pain. Doctor Clay McCord stood at the end of the bed, talking in a low voice, encouraging Beauty. Carrie didn't have to ask to know she was in the middle of delivering her baby.

Dropping her reticule, she washed her hands. "What do you want me to do, Doctor?"

Glancing up, Clay nodded toward Hawke. "Of course." Touching the deputy's arm, she got his attention. "Let's get you a chair in the front. Doctor McCord or I will get you once your baby arrives."

Hawke shook his head, features set. "I won't leave her."

"Mr. DeBell—"

"It's all right, Carrie. Hawke can stay, but don't you go fainting on me." Clay chuckled at the look of disgust on his friend's face. "Dampen a compress for him to wipe Beauty's forehead and face."

Carrie didn't have to ask to know Clay wanted to give Hawke something more to do while holding his wife's hand.

Hawke stroked hair off Beauty's forehead, bending down next to her ear. "It's going to be all right, sweetheart." Her smile changed to a grimace before she gritted her teeth.

Clay nodded at Carrie before focusing on his patient. "I want you to push when I tell you, Beauty."

Steeling herself, she squeezed Hawke's hand, waiting for the doctor. Her husband's steady gaze, the love in his eyes, lulled her into a sense of peace.

"Push." Clay's command, accompanied by another sharp pain, had her bearing down. "Again, Beauty."

An agonized groan sounded from deep in Beauty's throat. Long seconds passed before the pressure left her body, relief flooding through her. Closing her eyes, they popped open at a baby's cry.

"It's a boy." Clay grinned while working with Carrie to clean up the newborn.

Wrapping him in a small blanket, she cradled the tiny infant, moving to the side of the bed. "He's perfect." Carrie set the baby in Beauty's waiting arms.

A tired smile stared down at the scrunched, red face. Still, Beauty had never seen anything more gorgeous. Lifting her gaze to Hawke, she saw a tear slide down his face.

Carrie stirred a pinch of sugar into a cup of coffee, watching the traffic on the street through the boardinghouse's window. Another storm had formed early, snowing without pause throughout the day.

She'd planned to walk the short distance home after the clinic closed. Exhausted, and unwilling to suffer another meal of Georgina's, she'd chosen to eat at Suzanne's.

"Hope you can eat all of this." Rose Keenan, the town school teacher and one of the mail order brides, set a full plate in front of Carrie.

"I didn't know you still worked here."

Pulling out a chair, Rose sat down next to her. "It's not often. Only when Suzanne needs extra help."

Carrie touched the edge of her plate. "Have you eaten? There's more than enough for both of us."

"Thank you, but I ate not long after school ended. You'll love the chicken fricassee. It's the best I've ever had." Standing, she set the chair back in place. "I need to get back to work. I'm hoping to save enough for a horse."

"A horse? I didn't know you could ride."

Rose smiled, waving a hand in the air. "I can't."

Chuckling, Carrie took a bite of her supper, humming in satisfaction. Rose was right. It was the best fricassee she'd ever eaten. She thought of Griffin, wondering what he was doing. Working late? Having another meal at the

Eagle's Nest? Could he be courting someone? After visiting with pie the night before, she doubted the last.

She'd spent little time around him since his arrival in Splendor with Bram and Thane MacLaren. There'd always been something about Griffin causing Carrie to keep her distance. If he hadn't been Francesca's law partner, she doubted she'd ever be in his company.

Until last night, he'd paid little attention to her...or Georgina. The last made her wonder if his visit was due to an interest in her friend.

Taking another bite, her gaze wandered back outside. The storm had worsened while she'd been inside the boardinghouse. She couldn't see the Western Union and stagecoach office across the street, or the Wild Rose Saloon next door to it.

"More coffee?" Rose stood next to her, although her gaze was locked on the blizzard outside. "Appears I'm going to be here longer than planned."

Glancing around, Carrie saw everyone staring outside. "I doubt anyone will be leaving for a while, Rose."

She found herself hoping Georgina was safe at their small house. Then her thoughts moved again to Griffin. He lived a few houses away and across the street from them. She'd often watched as he walked past their place late in the evening. Back straight, shoulders squared, he always appeared confident and fully in control.

Carrie had heard about the shooting at Finn's Saloon. The story was Griffin had drawn on and killed a man who'd fired at him, and wounded two others. Dutch

McFarlin had arrived to stop a fourth man from killing Griffin.

At one point, she believed Dutch would ask to court her. To Carrie's relief, he hadn't. Smart and handsome, the deputy didn't stir her interest enough to spend a lifetime together.

The sound of the front door crashing open had most of those in the restaurant pushing away from their tables. The men stood. Those with guns slipped them from their holsters.

Griffin and Bram brushed snow from their coats before turning toward the dining room. Their bodies stilled at the sight of the guns.

"Hell, Griff. You didn't tell me they wanted to run us out of town." Bram meant his comment as a joke, but neither of them laughed.

A short, rotund man holstered his gun, holding up a hand. "Sorry, boys." The others in the room followed his lead before sitting back down.

Carrie's stomach shifted, chest tightened at the sight of Griffin. The reaction bothered and surprised her. Of the few times they'd been around each other, not once did she recall feeling the odd sense of unease mixed with a strange anticipation.

"What's wrong with you?" she whispered to herself, hoping no one else heard.

Suzanne walked toward them, holding out her hands to take their coats. "Give me those and pick a table. I'll bring you coffee."

"Thanks, Suzanne." Griff looked around, his gaze landing on Carrie. A slow smile lifted the corners of his mouth as his feet moved without much encouragement. Removing his hat, he fingered the brim. "Miss Galloway. Do you know Bram MacLaren?"

"Of course she does, Griff. How are you, lass?"

"Fine, Mr. MacLaren." She turned toward the window to see the storm hadn't let up.

"May we join you?"

Her attention shifted back to Griffin. "Please. I'd enjoy the company while waiting for the storm to pass."

"It may be a while." Taking a seat next to her, he thanked Suzanne for the coffee before returning his attention to Carrie. "I enjoyed spending time with you and Miss Wise last evening." He ignored the flash of interest in Bram's eyes.

"So did we. The pie was wonderful. Thank you again for sharing it with us."

"It was more than I could eat. Since you're on my way home, I decided to stop."

Her enthusiasm waned a little at his words. Of course he hadn't come by for any reason other than finding willing participants to share the pie.

"How are you doing, Mr. MacLaren?"

"Fine, lass. Waiting for spring to arrive." Bram sipped his coffee, a brow lifting at Griffin.

"And your wife?"

Features softening, a grin appeared. "Selina is doing well. Works as hard as any of the men on the ranch."

"From the little I know about her, she has a talent for working with horses."

"That she does, lass."

"Are you gentlemen ready to order?" Rose listened, answered questions, then returned to the kitchen.

"Any excitement at the clinic today?" Griffin held his cup, watching her over the rim.

"Beauty had her baby."

Both men's eyes widened.

"A beautiful boy. Hawke refused to leave her side." Emotion clogged her throat. She'd never forget the look of complete love on Hawke's face, as well as the lone tear rolling down his face.

"Have they given the lad a name?" Bram asked.

"Not yet. Hawke's staying with Beauty and the baby at the clinic until Doctor McCord gives his permission to go home. I'm so happy for them."

The three finished their suppers in silence, Carrie casting furtive glances outside. The storm had calmed some, enough to see a completely dark sky. She should've gone home after leaving the clinic. Looking to her side, she saw Griffin watching her.

"What is it?" Using her napkin, she dabbed at the corners of her mouth.

"I'll walk you home."

Shoulders sagging in relief, she gave a grateful smile. "Thank you, Mr. MacKenzie." Her gaze moved to Bram. "Where will you be staying?"

"At the St. James. I've supplies to get tomorrow before heading back to the ranch. Are we ready to leave?"

Standing, Griffin pulled out Carrie's chair while Bram placed money on the table for all three meals. Retrieving coats, Griffin assisted her into the long, woolen tweed with a hood he'd seen her wear in cold weather. He guessed it to be a purchase made before she'd left New York a few years earlier.

The wind picked up as they left the shelter of the restaurant. Offering his arm, Griffin tugged her to his side as they made their way along the boardwalk to the St. James. Not surprising, they encountered no one else on the short journey to the hotel.

Nor were they surprised to see the Dixie and Finn's doing robust business. The Dixie and Wild Rose were owned by Gabe Evans and Nick Barnett. Neither offered entertainment other than what could be had downstairs. Finn's, on the other hand, was known for providing much more in the upstairs bedrooms.

Passing the Emporium, Carrie glanced inside, seeing nothing except complete darkness. Owned by Clay McCord's wife, Olivia, and Dom Lucero's wife, Josie, the store offered upscale goods not available at the town's general store. Carrie had been saving for a beautifully carved box in the front window, hoping to purchase it by summer.

The sound of horses drew their attention. Stopping, the three glanced around, noting the deserted street. The neighing sounded again, this time accompanied by hooves beating on the frozen ground.

"There." Griffin pointed toward the narrow opening between the millinery shop and bank in time to see four men, each on their own horse.

"What do you think..." Carrie began, then stopped as her gaze landed on the front of the bank. "The window."

Griffin and Bram turned from watching the riders retreat south. A large opening stared back at them, shards of glass spread out over the boardwalk and onto the street. Carrie tightened her hold on Griffin's arm, her face, full of alarm, lifted toward his.

"They robbed the bank!"

Chapter Four

Gabe surveyed the gaping hole in the bank's front window. The robbery had been simple, yet brilliant. Ride into town at night using the storm for cover. It was now eight at night, and the storm had taken a turn for the worse. He wondered how often the outlaws had done the same in other towns.

Two of his deputies, Cash Coulter and Beau Davis, flanked him, expressions grim. Both had their collars turned up, hats pressed tight to their heads to ward off the cold. They'd spent the last hour talking with anyone who might have seen the outlaws. The storm had kept everyone inside, and with the wind, no one heard or saw the men who'd broken into the bank.

Inside, bank president, Horace Clausen, assessed the loss. He cared little about the broken window. The stolen money vexed him.

Several years earlier, the banker had the foresight to order a second safe. Installed behind a false wall, few knew of its existence. Gabe, Cash, Beau, and Nick Barnett were the four men Horace trusted with the information.

Gabe turned at the sound of a wagon approaching. Silas Jenks, owner of the lumber mill, drew to a stop in front of the bank.

"Got the wood you ordered, Gabe." Jumping down, he walked to the back of the wagon to retrieve what was needed to secure the opening. Beau and Cash joined him, and within a few minutes, the wagon was empty.

"What can we do, Gabe?" Morgan Wheeler, one of the three newest deputies, didn't wait for an answer. Bending down, he picked up a hammer and nails someone had placed under the broken window. Fellow deputies, and his good friends, Jonas Taylor and Tucker Nolan, lifted a large piece of lumber, fitting it against the opening.

"You're already doing it. I'm going inside to talk with Horace."

Touching the brim of his hat, Morgan began pounding the wood into place. "Heck of a thing. My guess is I was a block away when the outlaws broke the glass."

Jonas steadied the piece of wood. "I was in the Wild Rose. Didn't hear anything."

Tucker pressed his lips together, jaw tight. He'd been on duty, but decided to have supper at McCall's. The restaurant was just two buildings away from the bank. He'd heard nothing.

"Griff told Gabe there were four riders. They headed south. We should be searching for them," Tucker said.

Morgan stopped pounding a nail, looking over at Tucker. "Doubt we'd have much luck tonight. Storm's gotten worse."

Adjusting his stance, Jonas nodded. "It's going to be darn hard to track them in this weather. It's been about two hours. Any signs will be long gone by the time the storm clears."

Continuing to secure the wood over the broken window, Morgan found himself agreeing with Jonas. The money was gone, as were those who stole it.

Carrie held her cup of tea with both hands as she stared outside. Three stoves burned in the small, two bedroom house, but a chill continued to run through her. Georgina hadn't emerged from her room since Carrie's return. She was grateful for the quiet.

Lowering herself into a chair, her thoughts went to the four outlaws. It had all happened too fast for her to get a good look at any of them. But there was something...

Resting her head against the back of the chair, she closed her eyes. Forcing herself to relax, Carrie thought about the minutes before the riders appeared, hoping to remember anything useful.

She, Griffin, and Bram had been yards away from the St. James when something drew her attention across the street. The storm had cleared enough to see the broken window. Then the riders emerged from between the bank and millinery. Four horses. Four men.

Carrie's eyes popped open. A clear image of one rider had her sitting up. A frightened gaze had locked on hers. What had Carrie sitting up straight was the memory of long, blonde hair flowing from beneath a flat-brimmed felt hat.

Three men and one woman. Jumping up, she grabbed her coat, rushing outside. Pulling the hood over her head, Carrie hurried toward the bank, mindful of the ice and snow.

Slipping through the narrow opening between the bank and Griffin's law office, she heard voices. Relief flooded her. She recognized Gabe's, then Griffin's. Walking toward them, she realized no one noticed her, their attention on the front of the bank.

"Mr. MacKenzie."

Griffin whipped around, eyes widening when he saw her. "Miss Galloway. What are you doing here?"

Within minutes of her spotting the broken window, Griffin had escorted her home while Bram went for the sheriff.

Glancing at Gabe, she cleared her throat. "I remembered something about the riders."

Griffin's features softened. "All right."

"We know there were four outlaws. I assumed they were all men. I'm now certain one was a woman."

Gabe stepped closer. "Why?"

"Long, blonde hair flowed from under her hat as they rode away."

Griffin touched her arm. "Are you sure about that?"

Catching her lower lip between her teeth, she thought for a moment before nodding. "Yes."

Griffin rubbed his chin. "Have you heard of a gang which includes a woman, Gabe?"

"There've been two or three with women, but the ones I know about are south of here. Did you notice anything else, Miss Galloway?"

"Only the horses."

"What about them?" Gabe asked.

"They weren't what I expected outlaws to ride."

"Tell me about them."

"Even with the snow falling, I could tell each of the horses was a magnificent animal. Appaloosas is my guess."

Gabe lifted a brow. "All four?"

"Yes. I know because a friend in New York bred them. We rode together as often as possible before I left for Splendor. I hope this helps you find them."

Griffin set a hand on her shoulder. "This is excellent information, Miss Galloway."

She let out a breath. "I'd appreciate it if you'd call me Carrie. Both of you."

"If you'll call me Griff."

"All right."

"Feel free to call me Gabe. Or sheriff."

"Excellent. I'm going back to my house. I'll let you know if I think of anything else."

"Are you good here, Gabe?"

"We've done all we can for now, Griff. Thank you for getting me the new information, Carrie." Touching the brim of his hat, Gabe turned back to the bank.

"May I walk you back home...Carrie?"

"I'd like that, Griff." Slipping her arm through his, he tucked her close.

Griffin knew the walk wouldn't take as long as he hoped. If the snow had subsided, he would've suggested a longer stroll around town. Ten minutes wasn't near enough with the beautiful woman.

"How is the partnership with Francesca going?" Carrie winced at what she thought might be an inappropriate question.

Looking down at her, a grin tipped up one corner of his mouth. "Quite well. She's a remarkable woman."

"Yes, she is." If Francesca wasn't happily married to Zeke Boudreaux, Carrie might've felt a stab a jealousy. An odd reaction, as she and Griffin weren't a couple.

"Did you always want to be a nurse?"

"Not always. At sixteen, I witnessed a terrible accident. Two carriages crashed into each other. Both were filled with women and children. If it hadn't been for two women who were nearby, most of them would've died. They were nurses." She looked up at him. "One was Rachel Pelletier. She's the reason I decided to become a nurse."

"The reason you came to Splendor."

"Yes, but it's more than that. I trained under her in New York. We became good friends. When she sent the telegraph about joining her, it happened to be a good time for me."

Turning onto their street, Griffin slowed the pace, wanting to prolong their time together. "I'd like to hear that story sometime."

Stopping at her front door, he turned toward her. "Miss Galloway, would you allow me to call on you?"

Although she'd found herself hoping he'd show an interest, the request caught her unprepared. It must've shown on her face. To his credit, Griffin smiled.

"Have I surprised you?"

"Well...yes. We've spent so little time together."

"Which is why I'm interested in calling on you." Reaching out, he touched her cheek, a gesture he knew was premature.

"I would enjoy learning more about you, Griff. So, yes, I'd very much like it if you called on me."

"Would tomorrow for supper suit?"

"Yes, it would."

"Excellent. I'll come by at six." Bending, he brushed a chaste kiss across her cheek.

Feeling her face heat at the contact, she swallowed, giving a slow nod. "I'll look forward to it." Opening the door, she slipped inside, missing his last words.

"Not as much as I will."

Chapter Five

Dirty Dave Dugan dipped his head against the increasing wind, shivering from the bone-deep chill. Tugging on the reins, he guided his horse along the narrow trail leading to Big Pine, Montana.

The storm stalled his progress on his journey from Moosejaw to the territorial capital. He'd heard stories about Big Pine, specifically the longtime sheriff, Parker Sterling. Dave's cronies in the Dakotas warned him to be careful showing his face in the burgeoning western town.

The older, taciturn lawman shouldn't be underestimated, they'd told him. Those who did might not live long enough to regret it. Shivering, and at least five miles away from Big Pine, Dave didn't much care about the sheriff. His thoughts centered on staying alive.

Feeling the reins grow taut, he turned. "Can't stop now, Scarlett."

The mare shook her head, digging her back hooves into the hard ground. Dave knew from experience he'd have a hard time getting the horse to move. Securing his hat with his other hand, he searched for some place to bunk down for the night, doubting there'd be much in the stark desert of eastern Montana.

Dave had waited to leave the Dakotas until the final months of winter. His bad luck, the snow had come later than usual.

"I shoulda known, Scarlett. Next time, we'll start out before Thanksgiving." A bark of laughter burst from his parched lips. "Hell, next year at this time we'll be in California. Maybe San Diego. They don't know what snow is down there."

The laughter faded when a strong gust of wind forced him to his knees. Falling forward, he cursed loud and long. Swiping a hand over his face, he cussed again. His long, lush mustache lay frozen against his roughened skin.

Shoving up, his knees buckled when Scarlett stepped backward, but he righted himself before landing on his backside. Struggling to stay upright when another gust of wind hit him, Dave stumbled to his saddle, gripping the saddlehorn.

He'd counted on the storm passing and being in Big Pine long before now. The original idea included a week in the territorial capital before riding on to Splendor. It wasn't his ultimate destination. Dave planned to be playing cards and sipping whiskey in a San Francisco saloon long before the snows fell next winter. First, he had to stay alive long enough to reach Big Pine.

Splendor

Griffin read the contract a third time, still not satisfied with the corrections already made. An older couple living three miles south of town had made the hard decision to sell their ranch and move to Kansas City to live near their daughter.

The buyers were two men he knew well. Hex and Zeke Boudreaux, both deputies in Splendor, had been looking for well over a year. They wouldn't move in right away. They planned to build a second house not far from the original homestead, each brother taking one.

Riding out with them a week earlier, Griffin understood their desire to buy. People were moving to western Montana at a rapid pace, buying whatever served their needs. This property covered two thousand acres, a thousand apiece, of prime land with excellent water and a fair amount of trees. More than enough for the men who planned to work their ranches when not performing their duties in town.

Griffin had his sights on property a mile north of town in an area the locals called Rocky Basin. At two hundred acres, it wasn't large enough for a cattle ranch, but he could breed horses. He'd been talking with the owners for months. They'd forged a good deal. All he had to do was sign the papers. Completing the deal with the Boudreaux brothers would provide the last of the funds needed to close on his own property.

Finishing his last review, making two more notes, Griffin sat back in his chair. Satisfied, he gathered the papers. Back in Conviction, he'd had three legal secretaries. In Splendor, he and Francesca relied on a recently hired young man who arrived in Splendor a month before Christmas.

Damon Broom had little experience, making up for it with an eagerness Griffin and Francesca appreciated. He'd boarded the train in Omaha, deciding to take the stage to Big Pine, then continuing on to Splendor. Francesca and her husband, Zeke, had met him while dining at the Eagle's Nest.

Walking down the stairs, he set the papers on Damon's desk, checking the time on the clock which hung on a nearby wall. Noon. Six hours until he'd be escorting Carrie to supper. The surge of excitement surprised him. It had been a long time since he'd felt more than a passing interest in a woman.

The front door swung open, Gabe stepping into the office. "Do you have a few minutes, Griff?"

"I do. Let's go upstairs." He wondered what would bring the sheriff to his office. The other times he'd been with his wife, Lena, or his business partner, Nick Barnett. "Have a seat, and tell me what brought you here."

"Nick and I are buying the Imperial Hotel in Big Pine. It's located next to the Glacier Saloon."

"How's business at the Glacier?"

Gabe chuckled. "Better than expected. Much of it is because of Paul. He was a good choice for managing it."

"So you're buying the Imperial. Do you have the details?"

Reaching into a pocket, Gabe handed Griffin a folded piece of paper. Opening it, he scanned the particulars, nodding as he read. Finishing, he didn't try to hide a grin.

"Darn good deal, Gabe. How'd you manage it?"

"The owners live in Denver and want out. Paul heard about their decision to get out of Big Pine, and passed the information along to us. We'll need to do some work on the hotel and find a manager, but we believe it's a good investment."

Griffin wanted to laugh. Everything Gabe and Nick did became a huge success.

"This won't be a difficult contract. Give me three days. I want Francesca to review it." He stood, extending his hand to Gabe.

"You may not know, but Chan and two other men escorted Purdy Dwyer and the two other outlaws to Big Pine for trial. Doubt we'll hear from them in a long time."

Letting out a breath, Griffin nodded. "Thanks, Gabe. I'm glad to hear they're no longer in Splendor. Morty Gallant was vicious, but Purdy was twice as bad. The man never needed a reason to kill."

Rubbing his jaw, Gabe dipped his head before leaving.

Staring into her armoire, Carrie's gaze moved over the dresses, blouses, and skirts. The green one she'd worn at Shane and Angela's wedding drew her attention. The color went well with her auburn hair and blue eyes bordering on green.

Reaching out, she pulled it over her head, realizing the buttons in back required help. Georgina was having supper with Rose at the boarding house. Francesca and

Zeke lived next door. If she hurried, there might be time to get there and back before Griffin arrived.

Grabbing a coat, she slipped one arm into a sleeve, then froze at the knock on her front door. Biting her lower lip, she weighed what to do next. Several more knocks made the decision for her.

Securing the coat around her, she put on her best smile while drawing the door open. "Good evening, Mr...Griffin. Won't you come in?"

"Hello, Carrie." Cocking a brow, his gaze moved over her. "It appears you're ready to go."

Glancing down, she gave a slight shake of her head. "There is something I must do. Would you like coffee while you wait?"

"Not right now. Go ahead and finish. Take as much time as you need."

Giving a weak smile, she returned to her bedroom, stopping by the wardrobe. Removing the coat, she reached behind her, fumbling with the lowest buttons for several minutes before closing five. Doing the same behind her neck, she worked her way down. This time, four buttons were secured. Knowing there were at least six more, she tried again.

Perspiration beaded on her upper lip and brow after several attempts without success. Trying once more, she dropped her hands in frustration.

"Darn."

"Did you say something, Carrie?"

She glared at the door, wondering how he'd heard her. "No. Trying to finish."

"Do you need help?"

Did she? Shaking her head, she turned to look at the back of her dress in the mirror. From her position, she still counted six buttons. No matter how she tried, they were six she couldn't reach.

Keeping her coat on during supper wouldn't be acceptable. "What now?"

Carrie knew she could change into a different dress, but wasn't certain about releasing the already closed buttons. There was a solution, although not a good one.

Taking quiet steps toward the door, Carrie thought about her options, knowing she searched for a miracle. Swallowing her pride, she opened the door, peeking out.

"Um..."

"Yes?"

Letting out a breath, she stepped into the living room. "I might need some help."

Standing, his lips twitched as he approached her. "With what?"

Not meeting his gaze, she began backing into her bedroom, stopping when he settled a hand on her shoulder. He'd been with enough women to realize how tricky getting dressed and undressed could be.

"What do you need, Carrie?"

Feeling her face flush, she closed her eyes, not meeting his intense gaze. "The, um...buttons."

"Do you need me to close them?"

A pained expression crossed her face before she nodded. "It's not appropriate."

Coughing to hide a chuckle, he gripped a shoulder. "Turn around."

"I..."

Lifting a brow, he tugged on her shoulder. "Turn around, Carrie."

Doing as he asked, she shot furtive glances over her shoulder. She could feel his warm fingers through her chemise, the contact prompting her to suck in a breath. Closing her eyes, she counted the seconds. It took less than a minute to accomplish what had evaded her.

"All done."

Without looking at him, she rushed into her bedroom, closing the door. Hearing soft chuckles, she groaned, covering her face with both hands. As a nurse, her duties sometimes included cutting off men's or women's clothing in order to treat a wound. She'd never felt a bit of embarrassment.

This was quite different. It had nothing to do with being injured. Her stupidity at not foreseeing the problem closing the buttons irked her.

Carrie had wanted to impress him. Well, she did. Griffin probably thought her a simpleton.

Checking herself in the mirror, she picked up her reticule, releasing a slow breath. Squaring her shoulders, Carrie opened the door. Griffin stood near one wall, studying the only picture she owned of her family in New York.

"Are these your parents?"

Relief swept through her. Griffin had already forgotten the fiasco with her buttons.

"Yes. They're the ones on the right. The couple on the left are my aunt and uncle. Father's brother."

"Do you have brothers or sisters?"

"I have a brother who's ten years older. He works in Baltimore and isn't married. I also have twin sisters. They're four years older and both are married. One still lives in New York, the other in Boston. What about you?"

Shifting to look at her, he snagged her coat from a hook by the door. "Two sisters. Both married. Are you ready?" Holding up her coat, he closed the topic. She wondered what he hadn't said.

In their brief time together, Carrie already knew Griffin MacKenzie had secrets. If he gave her time, she was determined to discover each one.

Chapter Six

A smile crossed Griffin's face early the next morning as he passed Carrie's house. The evening had been entertaining and enlightening. She'd been easy to be around, curious, and interesting. Few women he'd known had the ability to see the humor in their actions. Carrie had no problem laughing at her own missteps, although Griffin had assured her closing the last six buttons hadn't been a blunder.

By the time he escorted her home, he'd learned a great deal about Miss Carrie Galloway. All of it leaving him with a desire to learn more. Griffin found her enchanting, more so than any woman he'd met in years.

If the weather was on his side, they'd take a ride to Rocky Basin on Saturday. The basin was located within the two hundred acres he planned to purchase soon. The current owners, clients of the law firm, moved to Salt Lake City with no plans to return.

A door opening and closing had him turning around. Carrie walked down the steps. She wore a scuffed pair of boots he hadn't seen before, navigating piles of snow and ice with ease. Glancing up, her gaze met his, a slight grin forming.

"Good morning, Griff."

"Morning, Carrie. On your way to the clinic?" Turning around, he held out his arm, which she took.

"Yes. There are days I wish the distance wasn't so short." She nodded toward the clinic. "Today isn't one of them."

Chuckling, he slowed to avoid a patch of dark ice. "Would you care to join me for lunch?"

"I'd love to. It will depend on what is going on at the clinic. If the doctors need me, lunch would be delayed."

"I'll wait if needed." Stopping by the clinic's entry, he felt a pang when she slipped her arm from his. "Shall I come by at noon?"

"That would be fine. Georgina prefers to have her lunch at eleven."

Waiting until she walked up the steps to the front door, he couldn't stop a grin. "I'll see you soon, Carrie."

Giving a sharp nod, she opened the door to enter the clinic.

Carrie leaned her back against the closed door, her heart pounding. A few minutes around Griff and she felt lightheaded, her breath coming in short puffs. No man had ever triggered this reaction, not even Shane Banderas, whom she liked a great deal.

These feelings for Griff were different, deeper, which was ridiculous given the slight amount of time they'd spent together. Convincing herself the excitement of breaking her routine of work and spending each evening

43

at home were the reasons for the odd sensations, she pushed away from the door.

Hearing someone cough, she glanced around the waiting area, wincing when her gaze landed on a mother with two young children. Removing her hat and coat, she walked to them, kneeling down in front of a little boy she guessed to be five.

"Hello. I'm Nurse Galloway. What's your name?"

Instead of answering, he buried his head in his mother's skirts. "His name's Teddy." She stroked his head, worry etched on her face. "He's had a cough for about a week. It's getting worse, not better."

Reaching up, Carrie touched his face, feeling a warmth more pronounced than normal. "How long has Teddy been running a temperature?"

The young woman looked away before answering. "Four days. I've done all I know to break it. My husband said we don't have money for a doctor, but I'm afraid of what will happen if the fever and coughing don't stop." Continuing to stroke her son's head, she swiped at a tear before meeting Carrie's sympathetic gaze.

"Does he know you're here?"

"No. I don't know what he'll do when he finds out."

Features turning fierce, Carrie stood. "Would he hurt you or the children?"

The woman's eyes widened. "Never. He'll worry more than he already does. Money is tight, and will be until we can sell our crops to some of the smaller ranchers. I've stretched what we have as far as I can, but..." Swiping at another tear, she lifted her chin. "Teddy getting better is more important right now."

"Let me get the doctor and prepare the examination room. I'll be right back."

Hurrying up the stairs, she heard voices from one of the examination rooms down the hall. Hanging up her coat and hat, she walked toward the room, stopping when a burst of loud cursing spilled into the hall.

"Enoch, you've got to hold still while I remove the boil."

"Hurts something awful, Doc."

"Trust me. If I don't remove it, the pain will get much worse. Do you want some whiskey?"

"No. Let's get it done."

Rapping on the door, she opened it an inch. "Doctor McCord, do you need my help?"

"Not right now. I'd rather you keep watch downstairs, Carrie."

"There is a woman with two young children. The boy has been sick for a week. His mother says he's had a fever for four days."

"Please show them into a room and start running a cold bath. This shouldn't take long. Right, Enoch?"

She could hear the older man's heavy sigh. "I sure hope not."

Closing the door, she hurried downstairs, the fluttering in her stomach from seeing Griffin forgotten.

"You're in a good mood today, Griff." Francesca Boudreaux, several papers in her hand, looked across his desk.

"I'm in a good mood every day, Frannie."

"True. Today, though, you have a sparkle in your eyes. Who is she?"

Looking up from the contract he'd been reading, he set down the pen. "What makes you believe it's about a woman?"

Shrugging, her lips twitched. "Well, I did hear you escorted Carrie to supper at the St. James."

Mouth twisting into a grimace, he gave a slow shake of his head. "Sometimes, this town is too darn small."

Laughing, she handed him the papers. "All the time, Griff. The town thrives on gossip. I feel obligated to warn you about not hurting Carrie."

"Not my intention."

"Men never intend to hurt women. It just happens. Carrie is an amazing person and a good friend. I'm asking you to be careful how you proceed."

Griffin glanced down at the papers on his desk for a long moment before raising his gaze to Francesca. "I hold Carrie in the highest esteem. She's important to me, Frannie. That's all I'm willing to say."

Studying his face, she offered a nod. "All right. That's good enough for me." She pointed to the papers she'd handed him. "The contract between Gabe, Nick, and the current owners of the Imperial Hotel. Also, the contract for the Boudreaux brothers to purchase the property south of town. There's nothing I'd change on either one."

"Good. Gabe and Nick are ready to move forward. I'll take the contracts to the jail. I might get lucky and find one of the Boudreaux brothers and Gabe."

"What about the land you want to purchase?"

"Everything is ready. As soon as the Boudreaux purchase closes, I'll finalize my deal. Carrie and I are riding out to Rocky Basin on Saturday. I'd like her to see it."

"So supper did go well."

Chuckling, he thought of his time with Carrie. "Well enough, Frannie."

"Must've been. Have you ever taken another woman to Rocky Basin?"

"Not that I recall."

Smirking, she shook her head as she walked back toward her office.

Dirty Dave stumbled, his face slamming against the frozen ground. Stunned, he didn't feel the reins slipping through his fingers, or hear hooves plodding past him toward the buildings half a mile away.

Groaning, he rolled to his back. His head throbbed, entire body ached. Blinking, he drew in a deep breath, letting it out in a rush of air. He thought of his horse and jumped up, regretting it when a wave of dizziness had him rocking on his feet.

Pressing fingers to his temples, he turned in a circle, shoulders relaxing at the sight of Scarlett. His mare stood not thirty yards away, staring at him as if waiting for Dirty Dave to hurry up.

Taking a step, he cursed at a sharp pain in his hip. It had never been the same after falling off Scarlett while in a drunken stupor. Doing his best to ignore the tenderness in his hip, the throbbing in his head, and aching body, he limped toward his horse.

Careful not to cause more pain, he placed a booted foot into the stirrup and swung his tired body into the saddle. Blowing out a breath, he slumped forward, then forced himself to straighten. He couldn't draw attention to himself when riding into Big Pine. After hearing about Sheriff Parker Sterling, he planned to spend little time in the territorial capital.

Reaching the edges of town, his gaze landed on the nearest saloon. Whiskey sounded real good. Next door was a boardinghouse, and across the street, a livery. Everything he needed without having to ride down the center of town. Or pass by the jail.

Leaving Scarlett at the livery, he secured a room at the boardinghouse for two nights, then walked straight into the saloon. He counted a total of six people, including the bartender. Not unusual for a little after noon.

"A whiskey." Lifting his head, he startled at the sight of himself in the large mirror mounted on the back wall of the bar.

Covered in dirt, dried blood on his face, he understood when the bartender rushed away after setting the whiskey in front of him. He probably smelled as bad as he looked.

Trail dust and mud-caked boots weren't unusual for most patrons of frontier saloons. Dirty Dave looked as if he'd been rolling in a pig sty, and was certain the stink carried throughout the room and outside. Not that he cared.

He'd get a bath at the boardinghouse, but not before filling his stomach with whiskey and a meal. "What you got to eat here?"

The bartender smirked. "Not much. Eggs, biscuits, and maybe bacon. I'd have to look in the back."

"I'll take whatever you have. And another whiskey."

It took an hour for his body to stop aching. His mind began going over his plan.

First on his list was to send a telegraph to the sheriff in Splendor to confirm the man he sought was still there. Next, he'd buy extra ammunition. Dave had started the trip light, figuring to get what he needed in Big Pine. Last, he'd buy new clothes, and get a shave and haircut, knowing he wouldn't be recognized in clothes more suitable for a banker or lawyer. A smile curved his lips. The man wouldn't know his fate until it stared him in the face.

"Here you are."

His mouth watered at the food the bartender set before him. "Where's your telegraph office?"

"This side of the street, a block down."

"Thanks."

Tucking into his meal, Dirty Dave felt a wave of satisfaction. *"It won't be long now, Willard. Not long at all."*

Chapter Seven

Judge Hoodoo Hardin ran a hand over his overly long, curly, red hair before smoothing his long, distinctive handlebar mustache. He couldn't recall a time he'd felt so helpless, and so damned alone. Being a widower didn't suit him. Eating alone, staring toward the street from the chair on his porch, hoping to see his wife returning from one of her many meetings. It had taken months to accept she truly was gone.

Staring down at the papers on his dining room table, he picked up a pen. Jaw clenched, Hoodoo signed the contract selling his house in Denver to a businessman who'd made a fortune importing silk, selling it to buyers throughout the country. The man had sold the family home in New York, and closed his accounts at Jay Cooke and Company.

From what Hardin had learned, the middle-aged man was considered a financial genius. The buyer had become uncomfortable with the enormous debt from the war, worthless greenbacks, and speculators who backed reconstruction with little knowledge of what he considered dire financial consequences.

Hoodoo didn't care about the man's reasons for cashing out and moving west. He had his own problems, and the time had come to face them.

The judge's wife had been killed in a shootout between rival gunmen several months earlier. Both gunmen escaped, but not before Hoodoo learned the identity of the one who murdered his wife.

His children had married and moved away years ago, eager to leave the dusty cow town. They hadn't even made it back for their mother's funeral. Hoodoo would never forgive them for what he saw as disrespect for the woman who'd brought them into the world.

Setting down the pen, he took one last look around the home his beautiful wife had created for her family. He'd looked forward to walking through the front door each evening, smelling supper cooking, and the music of his children's voices. He'd never thought the last years of his life would be barren to the point selling out, and leaving, was his only option in order to keep his sanity.

His gaze landed on the furniture they'd carefully chosen from the time he'd begun his law practice outside of Chicago. They'd hauled every piece with each move. Illinois, Missouri, Oklahoma, and finally Texas, where they settled for almost ten years before heading north to Colorado.

The years practicing law, and a sitting judge, included countless hours testing his skill with a six-shooter. More than one judge had been murdered after sentencing outlaws to hang or spend the rest of their lives in prison. Twice, he'd put those skills to use. Both times he'd been the one standing after the smoke cleared, earning him the reputation of being the gun-toting judge. He'd always thought the title less colorful than his actions merited.

Heart squeezing at leaving the house, furniture, and most of his family's belongings behind, he shoved out the front door. His horse and one pack animal had been loaded with what he couldn't leave behind. A few pictures, his wife's letters, and a scattering of mementos which meant a great deal to him, and nothing to anyone else.

Swinging into the saddle, Hoodoo rode through the center of town, waving to those he recognized. People he'd never see again. Cutting all ties was the only way he could leave his previous life behind.

The months ahead sprawled out before him. If all went as planned, he didn't expect to live into the following year. The prospect no longer bothered him. By January, he'd be back with his wife, content in her welcoming arms.

Isabella Dixon added a few dried apples to her husband's lunch, her heart pounding at what she suspected. Travis would be leaving soon for his job as a horse breeder and trainer for Dax and Luke Pelletier.

Leaving their home in town before dawn had become routine, as had his return after dark. He didn't mind the long ride to Redemption's Edge, or the hard work which came with his position. From the start, Travis had been determined not to use Isabella's wealth to put a roof over their heads and food on the table. They'd agreed to use her money to help purchase a house at some point, although he'd shown no interest in going forward with their plan.

Isabella didn't mind the delay. She preferred living in town, seeing her friends, taking care of the children when both parents worked. A craving for their own children continued to plague her, but she'd agreed to Travis's demand. If they married, he did not want children. It was stupid of her to go along, but she loved her husband dearly, and wanted marriage to the taciturn cowboy.

Now, all they had, the life they'd created, may be lost.

"I'll see you tonight." Travis took the lunch from her outstretched hand, dropping a kiss on her lips. "It's Friday. We should go to the boardinghouse or McCall's for supper."

Isabella drew in a breath, clasping her hands so tight the knuckles had begun to turn white. "Aren't you going to the Pelletiers' tomorrow?"

A tight smile lifted the corners of his mouth. "Dax ordered me to take the day off. Says I've been working too hard."

"You disagree?"

Looking away, he stared out the window of their rented house. "I work the same as everyone else. No need for me to be ordered to stay away."

Moving in front of him, Isabella placed her hands on his shoulders. "Two days together would be wonderful. Don't you think so?"

The tight muscles of his jaw relaxed, his eyes showing the warmth he felt at his wife's touch. "Yes, it would."

"Even with snow, we could ride out to the cabin you've considered buying. I could pack food."

Looking down, he couldn't miss the hope in her eyes. "That would be fine, sweetheart." Kissing her once more, Travis closed the door behind him, leaving Isabella alone with her thoughts.

Glancing at the wall clock Travis had given her the previous Christmas, she finished dressing, a cold ball of worry building in her stomach. Her destination wouldn't open for another hour. Another hour to worry about what she suspected, and what would happen when Travis learned the news.

Carrie straightened her coat, pulling the hood over her head. A light snow had begun as she ate her eggs and biscuit. The fact it hadn't worsened was a good sign. She hoped it wouldn't turn into a heavy storm, preventing Griffin from taking her to Rocky Basin.

Her last ride had been well before Thanksgiving to the Pelletier ranch. She and a few of her friends visited with Rachel, staying the night before returning to town. The sprawling ranch offered dozens of trails, and the opportunity to watch the ranch hands herd the cattle, and break wild horses. She'd loved every minute.

If she were honest, Carrie couldn't imagine a better life. She could also admit she envied Rachel a little, knowing in her heart, her future didn't include a similar life.

A brisk rap on the front door stopped her from finishing the last of her morning coffee. Opening the door, her eyes lit at the sight of Griffin, a thin blanket of snow covering his coat and hat.

"Good morning, Carrie. May I walk you to the clinic?"

"You should be careful, Griff. This might become a habit."

"I'm counting on it."

Closing the door, she slipped her arm through his. "Do you have a busy day?"

"Contracts, which may put me to sleep, and a brief meeting with Hex and Zeke Boudreaux. If all goes well with them, we'll be riding out to see the property they're purchasing south of town."

"I heard about the ranch from Francesca. She's excited and a little concerned about the distance from town. As your partner, I assume she's talked to you about it."

"Several times." Griffin wrapped his gloved hand over hers as they approached the clinic. "Frannie and I have come to an agreement on how work will be accomplished if she's unable to reach town. Zeke has assured her she'll be able to continue the law practice, and I agree." He chuckled. "I've no desire to take on the practice alone."

"Although you would if needed." Carrie slipped her hand from his, taking the steps to the clinic stoop.

"Until a partner could be found to take Frannie's place."

"Let's hope that never happens, Griff. Thank you for walking me to the clinic."

"My pleasure. Shall I come by at six to escort you to supper?"

Brows drawing together, she slanted her head to the side. "I don't recall us discussing supper."

"We just have." Touching the brim of his hat, he turned, missing the broad smile brightening her face.

Standing there a moment longer, she opened the door, stopping at the sound of her name. Isabella Dixon hurried toward her, all but bounding up the steps.

"Good morning, Carrie." Her face was flush, breath coming in short gasps. "Do you think the doctor would have time to see me this morning?"

"I'm certain he can, Isabella." Carrie opened the door, stepping aside so her friend could enter. "Why don't you wait here while I go upstairs and find him." Although subtle, she didn't miss how Isabella wrung her hands together, a nervous reaction Carrie wouldn't have associated with the elegant woman. Reaching the second floor, her gaze landed on Doctor Charles Worthington, Rachel's uncle and the man who started the clinic years before.

"Good morning, Carrie."

"Hello, Doctor. Isabella Dixon is downstairs. She seems quite, well...anxious."

"Isabella? I don't believe I've ever seen her out of sorts." Slipping into the new white coat a colleague from

New York sent to replace Worthington's black one, he nodded at Carrie to proceed him downstairs.

"Isabella, it's good to see you."

"It's been a long time, Doctor."

"I'm afraid Clare and I have taken to traveling whenever we're able. We will be leaving for a few months in San Francisco once a replacement for me is found. Clay is already communicating with a doctor in Denver and one in Cheyenne."

"I hope you aren't leaving Splendor for good."

"No. I'll be one of three doctors when in town. Let's go into the examination room so you may tell me what's bothering you."

Isabella touched her cheeks with an embroidered handkerchief, absorbing the tears she'd hoped to avoid. Her heart ached at confirmation of what she'd suspected.

"Would you like me to be there when you tell Travis?"

Staring down at the shaking hands in her lap, she shook her head. "Thank you, Doctor, but it's my responsibility."

"He's a good man, Isabella. Give him time to accept the news. I'm certain all will work out well."

She wasn't so sure. Travis had been firm before they married, and she'd agreed to his terms. He'd see this as a betrayal.

Sliding the handkerchief into a pocket in her skirt, she stood. "Thank you, Doctor Worthington."

"You're close to four months, Isabella. I expect to see you every few weeks unless you're experiencing pain."

"Of course."

Nodding at Carrie as she left the clinic, she forgot her plans to purchase meat and fresh bread from the shop on the way home. She walked right past people who called her name without acknowledging them.

For the first time since marrying Travis, Isabella feared for their future.

Chapter Eight

"How do I look?" Carrie turned in a circle in front of the cheval mirror, Georgina watching with her arms crossed. "I bought the riding skirt today at the Emporium. Josie showed me three. I fell in love with this one."

"It looks the same as any skirt. The brown color does go well with your boots and jacket. Is it new?"

Carrie sobered. "Samuel sent it to me for Christmas. I do wish my brother would travel out here for a visit. He'd love the mountains."

"Didn't you say he worked the docks? He must be doing well to afford a jacket as nice as yours."

Looking down, Carrie fingered the intricate embroidered pattern on the fine suede material, missing her brother more each day. She'd sent him a beautiful leather belt. Perhaps Samuel had thought he had to give her something of equal value. The jacket had to have cost much more than the belt.

Georgina hurried to the front door at the sound of a sharp rap, leaving Carrie to finish dressing. "Good morning, Griff. Please come inside. Carrie is almost ready. Would you like coffee?" She walked to the kitchen, moving the fabric wrapped food Carrie prepared onto their dining table.

"No coffee for me, Georgie."

Stepping to the window, she pulled back the curtains. "It's going to be a beautiful day for a ride. Are you certain it's safe with so much snow still on the ground?"

"Rocky Basin isn't much higher than Splendor, and we've had a few days of sun. I want to take the opportunity before the next set of storms begin." His attention shifted to Carrie, watching as she joined him. "You look...beautiful."

Gripping the sides of the skirt, she held the fabric out before touching the embroidered jacket. "Thank you. This was a present from my brother."

"You'll have to tell me more about him." Moving to the table, he picked up the wrapped food. "Are you ready?"

Her bright smile gave him the answer before she spoke. "I am quite ready."

It was a beautiful late February day with no signs of an approaching storm. The sun shone from a clear blue sky, dancing off millions of snow crystals on the ground.

Carrie had ridden into the wilderness and ranch lands outside of Splendor several times. Always in the summer when the biggest dangers were the four-legged kind. She'd never encountered a single bear, wolf, or puma, for which she was grateful.

She knew bear hibernated in the winter. Not so with wolves, who hunted in packs, or lone pumas, whose territory could spread for miles. Carrie didn't allow herself to worry about predators who might be lurking behind the cover of snow laden trees and bushes. She didn't want to think of anything except the man riding beside her.

"We aren't too far from Rocky Basin." Griffin shifted his gaze toward her. "Are you warm enough?"

The sun shone on her face, helping to keep her comfortable. Glancing down at her gloved hands, Carrie sighed, glad she'd decided to wear a knit cap under the hood of her coat.

"I feel wonderful. Who wouldn't on a day such as this?"

Griffin glanced at her without responding. Each smile she graced him with produced a punch to his gut never experienced with another woman. There was no doubt in his mind Carrie was who he'd marry. The knowledge should've alarmed him.

A man who'd figured to be a lifelong bachelor, Griffin had prepared himself for a quiet life, spending his evenings with friends, and eating alone most nights. Coming to Splendor with Bram and Thane MacLaren had changed his thoughts.

The number of single, attractive women had been unexpected. Carrie had caught his attention on their first night in town. It was Christmas Eve during one of the worst storms in Splendor history. It hadn't taken long to learn she held an interest in Shane Banderas. It was reciprocated for a time, until the love of his life showed up in town. Months had passed before Griffin felt she'd had time to rid Shane from her thoughts. Waiting had been a good decision.

"It's just up ahead." He gestured to a turn in the trail.

Before they reached it, voices came from their destination. One loud, the other pleading. Carrie recognized Isabella's voice.

"Oh, no."

Griffin shifted to look at her. "What?"

"I'm certain it's Travis and Isabella Dixon. She mentioned going on a picnic today, but I didn't know they were coming here. She has some, well...difficult news to tell her husband."

Kicking her horse, she rode ahead of Griffin, slowing at the sight of the couple a hundred feet away. Even from a distance, Carrie could see Travis's red face, the fisted hands on his hips. There was no doubt the announcement had not gone well.

Carrie knew the moment Isabella spotted her and Griffin. Their gazes locked, the older woman's face etched with pain.

Griffin rode closer. "Good morning, Isabella. Travis."

Back stiff, Travis tore his gaze from Isabella. "Griff."

"Is everything all right?" Carrie's question was directed at Isabella.

She shot a look at Travis before responding. "Yes. We're fine, Carrie."

"It's time we headed back to town." Travis grabbed the sack filled with food from its spot on a fallen log.

Securing it in a saddlebag, he motioned for Isabella to join him. Carrie had never seen her friend look more miserable. The strangest urge to slide to the ground, march up to Travis, and slap sense into him flashed through her. Staying put, she tempered her anger at the cowboy, knowing her thoughts wouldn't be welcome.

Riding up to Isabella, she leaned toward her. "I'll visit you on Monday."

Giving a slow nod, she kicked her horse when Travis ordered her to follow him.

Carrie watched them disappear around the bend of the trail, her heart heavy. Isabella was a wonderful woman, well-liked in Splendor, as was Travis. She'd never seen him angry. He adored his wife, would do anything for her. This would be a true test of his love.

"Do you know what's going on?"

Releasing a calming breath, Carrie continued to watch the trail. "Isabella is pregnant."

"Travis wasn't celebrating."

"No, he wasn't. Before they married, he made her agree to not have children. Doc Worthington told me Travis's wife and daughter were killed by raiders at the end of the war. He swore to never marry again. Then he met Isabella. It took him a long time to come to accept his feelings and marry her. Still, the doctor said he was adamant about never having children. I feel horrible for Isabella."

Dismounting, Griffin helped Carrie to the ground. They were fortunate most of the snow had melted under the heat of the sun over the last few days. Releasing the saddlebags, he took her hand, walking to where Isabella and Travis had placed their food.

"I don't know Travis well. He doesn't appear to be a man who'd leave."

Carrie hadn't considered he'd leave Isabella. "Men do that? Leave their pregnant wives?"

"It's been known to happen. They aren't able to deal with the responsibility of a wife *and* children. They ride out and never return."

"How does the woman and her children survive?"

He shook his head. "Sometimes they don't. Most times, the wife finds work wherever she can find it. Take in laundry, mending, cleaning houses. If all else fails, some work in the saloons."

Carrie crossed her arms, a shiver running through her. Seeing the horror on her face, he set down the food, wrapping his arms around her.

"I'm not that kind of man, Carrie. I'd never walk away from my wife or children. Do you understand?"

"I think so." Although she wasn't certain.

Leaning away, he lifted her chin with a finger. "You can trust me on that."

Bending down, he brushed a kiss across her lips. They were soft, moist, and all he knew they'd be. Straightening, he fought the urge to kiss her again.

Loosening his grip, he stopped when she looked back up at him. "Could you kiss me again?"

Amusement shown in his eyes. "It would be my pleasure."

Starting slow, he lowered his head again, the kiss a little more than chaste. When her hands moved up his arms to grip his shoulders, he kissed her again, this one creating a heat which shot through him. Coaxing her lips apart, he deepened the kiss, tentatively exploring the depths of her mouth.

Carrie's soft moan encouraged him and served as a warning. Lifting his head, he stole one last kiss before stepping back.

Eyes glassy, lips swollen, she stared at him. "Did I do something wrong?"

"You did everything right, sweetheart. That's why we have to stop."

Thinking about his words, her eyes widened. "Oh."

"You should know I'm serious about courting you, Carrie. I hope you feel the same."

A slow smile curved her lips. "I'm quite certain I do, Griff."

Big Pine

Dirty Dave leaned back in his chair, checking the cards in his hand. Picking up his glass, he sipped whiskey, waiting to see what the others at the table would do. The last few days had been a surprise. The cowboys who visited this particular saloon had experienced a run of bad luck at cards. Their losses became Dave's winnings.

Never leave while on a winning streak had become his motto, and his streak was solid. Rested, full of good food from a small restaurant a few doors away, Dave had no intention of leaving until his luck turned.

The telegram sent to Splendor had produced good news. The man he sought was there. After all this time, Dave was within a day's ride of the man who'd destroyed one life and ruined his.

"You gonna play, Dugan?"

Without much thought, he looked at the chips, tossing in a couple of his own while keeping his hand as it had been dealt. Resting his hands in his lap, he waited again, expecting he held winning cards.

One man after another folded, leaving him and one other to finish. Features unreadable, his eyes met his opponent's across the table. The two set down their cards, a smile played across Dave's face.

Reaching out with both hands, Dave scooped his winnings toward him, stopping when the saloon doors slammed open. Four outlaws, handkerchiefs over their faces and guns in their hands, stepped inside.

The tallest of the four moved forward. "Set your guns on the table and empty your pockets. Bartender, put all your money on the bar."

No one moved at first, all of them staring at the four. Dave's first reaction was that the voice didn't quite match the man's frame. Dismissing the odd thought, Dave glanced down at the gun in his holster, wondering if he could draw fast enough to the get the drop on the one who shouted the orders. When he looked up, the four outlaws had spread out, one of them shaking his head at Dave. All thoughts of keeping the money in his pockets fled.

"Do it, now!"

Mumbling curses, the men at the table tossed their money down. While three of the outlaws kept their guns trained on the patrons, the fourth stuffed money into a bag, thanking them as he walked past each.

Dave had never heard of an outlaw thanking those they stole from. His gaze followed the man around the table, locking on his hands. Slim fingers, trimmed nails, and pale skin. Nothing like any bandit he knew.

Finishing, the four backed toward the doors, three stepping outside. The tall one, gun still aimed at the gamblers, chuckled.

"Thank you, gentlemen. Don't try to come after us or you'll wish you hadn't. Enjoy your evening."

Dave fingered the handle of his six-shooter. He had no intention of following them. Most of his money was hidden in his room, making his loss small.

A couple of the men grabbed their guns and ran toward the doors, stopping when shots tore through the planks of the boardwalk. Jumping back, the pair cursed, making no move to go after them.

Dave rubbed his forehead, his mind going to the outlaw's voice, and hands too slender to be...

"Sonofabitch!" Hurrying to the front, he opened the bat-wing doors enough to see the four disappear out of town. Shaking his head, Dave grabbed his belly and laughed.

Chapter Nine

Splendor

"I don't understand, Travis." Isabella, one hand resting over her stomach, watched as her husband threw clothes into a satchel. "Why leave?"

Not slowing down, he didn't look at her as he tossed the last of his belongings in the bag. "I'm not leaving you. I need time to think, figure this out."

"What's there to figure out? I'm four months pregnant." Lowering herself onto the edge of the bed, she fought the fear enveloping her. "Please don't leave, Travis."

Closing the satchel, he walked to the dresser, opening a drawer. "There's plenty of money in this jar for a few weeks."

"I have my own money."

Rounding on her, he pinned her with an angry glare. "This is money I've earned. It's *ours*. I don't want you using your money for household expenses. I'll be staying in the bunkhouse at the Pelletier ranch. If you need me, send word. Don't ride out. I don't want you on a horse or wagon with ice on the trails."

Wrapping arms around her waist, she rocked enough to calm the ache in her chest. "When will you be back?"

Picking up the satchel, he walked toward the living room. "I don't know."

"A week, two weeks, a month? Don't you have some idea?"

He didn't turn around. "No."

"Do you plan to return, Travis?" She couldn't stop her voice from breaking.

He didn't respond.

Standing, she followed, determined not to break down before he left. "Is there nothing I can say to change your mind?"

Settling his hat on his head, Travis shifted toward her. "Not right now. I'm sorry, Isabella."

He stepped away when she reached out to touch him, the gesture like a knife to her heart.

Wrapping his gunbelt around his waist, he slid the six-shooter into the holster. She watched as he slipped into the heavy wool coat she'd given him for his last birthday.

Moving to the kitchen, she grasped a package wrapped in cloth. Walking toward him, she stopped a couple feet away, holding it out.

"The shortbread you like."

Reaching out, he tucked it under his arm. "Please take care of yourself."

"And the baby?"

His throat worked, but no words would come. Pulling their front door open, he stepped outside.

"I love you, Travis."

Pausing for a moment, his shoulders sagged, but he didn't face her. "Find Gabe if you need anything."

The sound of the door clicking shut broke her heart, crushing any hope she'd held that he'd stay. Stumbling backward, she grasped the back of a chair, steadying herself.

Isabella didn't know how long she stood in place, gaze locked on the closed door. Minutes passed, her breaths coming in short, painful gasps. He didn't want the baby. Didn't want her.

Back rigid, she lowered herself into the chair. She could go on alone, raise their child by herself if he didn't return. The death of her first husband, Arnott Boucher, had been difficult, but expected. He'd been twenty-five years older than Isabella, desiring companionship more than a true marriage. She'd loved Arnott's kind, giving nature. Her feelings for Travis were much deeper, more consuming. She didn't know how to a face a future without him.

They'd been married three and a half wonderful years. He'd been clear about his desire to never have children, and although she wanted a family, she'd relented to his wishes. Neither had considered what would happen if their methods of preventing a pregnancy didn't work.

Although he didn't say it, she knew Travis believed she'd betrayed their agreement. It hurt knowing his trust in her had been broken.

Tears leaked from her eyes, rolling down her cheeks. She didn't try to stop them.

The chime of the mantel clock drew her gaze to the time. Travis had been gone two hours. She'd hoped he think it through on the trail and turn around. The fact he didn't heightened her fear of him not returning.

Dabbing at the remaining dampness on her face, she forced herself to stand, then looked around as if she didn't know what to do next. Isabella realized her usual habits, such as stopping at the meat market and general store, weren't necessary. Without Travis, she had little to do.

Mondays meant visiting Lena Evans, her best friend since they were young. It had been Isabella who'd taken care of Jackson, Lena's son, when circumstances prevented his mother from being with him. For six years, the young boy lived with Arnott and Isabella, having rare contact with his mother. Lena and Gabe now had Emmaline. At two and a half, she kept her friends hopping.

Determined not to let Travis's decision rule her actions, Isabella returned to her bedroom to dress for the day. Slipping into a wool skirt and cotton blouse, she drew a brush through her lush dark hair, twisting it into a bun.

Staring at herself in the mirror, she didn't believe anyone would suspect she'd cried much of the morning. Pulling a wool scarf from her wardrobe, she wound it around her neck. Reaching for her coat, she hesitated at a hard knocking on her door. For an instant, her heart leapt, believing Travis may have come home. Then reality dashed her hope. He wouldn't knock.

Opening the door, her eyes widened at the sight of Lena, holding her daughter, Emma, and Suzanne with her son, Newt. "I was just leaving to meet you."

Neither woman said a word, walking past her into the living room. Setting the children down and removing their coats, they turned toward her, Lena speaking first.

"Gabe told me Travis left. He's going to stay at Redemption's Edge, but he didn't say why. What's going on?"

Unable to hide her grief, Isabella covered her face before bursting into tears. While Suzanne watched the children, Lena wrapped her arms around her closest friend.

Suzanne moved to answer the tapping on the door. Carrie stood outside, pulling her collar up to ward off the chill.

"Hello, Carrie. Please come inside."

Looking past Suzanne, her heart thudded. Isabella sat on the sofa next to Lena, crying in broken sobs. "Oh, no. I was so afraid this might happen."

"Do you know why Travis left?"

Nodding, Carrie shrugged out of her coat, going to kneel in front of Isabella. "I'm so sorry. What can I do?"

Red-rimmed eyes met hers, complete desolation on Isabella's face. "He left, Carrie."

"Because of the baby?" She ignored the sharp intakes of breath from Lena and Suzanne.

Clasping her hands in her lap, Isabella nodded. "Yes. I've never seen him so angry. He took almost all his belongings and left. Travis wouldn't tell me when, or if, he'd be back."

Lena gently rubbed her back, providing what support she could. "I know it's hard to accept right now, but Travis loves you. Perhaps he needs time to sort out his feelings. Redemption's Edge may be the best place for him right now. There isn't a man at the ranch who won't tell him leaving you and your baby isn't the answer."

Suzanne nodded her agreement. "Nick was in the jail when Travis stopped by this morning to speak with Gabe. He didn't say why he was staying away, just asked Gabe to check on you. If they'd known the reason for his leaving, you can be sure Travis would've heard more than he wanted."

"You shouldn't be here alone. You're welcome to come stay with Gabe and me. We could pack clothes and take them with us."

Isabella hadn't considered leaving. "What if Travis returns, Lena?"

Suzanne gave a derisive chuckle. "It would serve him right to come home and find you gone. The man needs to be hung by his feet until blood returns to his brain. The more I think about it, the more angry I get. Maybe we should let Reverend Paige know what's going on. He'll ride out there without us asking."

Isabella choked out a brittle laugh. "I don't think now is the right time."

Crossing her arms, Suzanne tapped a booted foot on the floor. "If he doesn't come back in a few days, then I think you should consider telling the reverend."

"Doc Worthington will want to know. Changes such as this can affect the baby." When Isabella's eyes grew wide, Carrie explained. "They're just discovering how much anxiety can affect a pregnancy. He isn't going to be pleased that Travis is causing you to worry. Do you mind if I tell him?"

"I'd appreciate it, Carrie. I'm not ready to talk about this to anyone else." Pressing the wrinkled handkerchief against the moisture lingering on her face, Isabella let out a shaky breath. "I may accept your invitation to stay with you and Gabe, Lena."

"Wonderful. We can get you moved right now."

"Not yet. I want to give him a few days to come home. If he doesn't return, or I don't hear from him by Thursday, I'll come for a few days." Staring at her hands, she lifted her gaze to Carrie. "Would you mind asking Griffin if he or Frannie would come see me? Since I don't know what Travis will do, I want to make provisions for the baby."

Brows crinkling, Carrie stood. "Of course I'll ask. But what kind of provisions are you considering?"

Clearing her throat, Isabella squared her shoulders, lifting her chin. "If anything happens to me, and Travis refuses to accept his child, then I want to have alternatives in place."

The room quieted, no one wanting to consider anything happening to Isabella, or Travis not claiming his child.

Lena reached over, taking Isabella's hand. "Maybe you should speak with Hawke. He didn't want a family after losing his wife and sons. Then Beauty became pregnant. Travis might listen to him."

"I'll consider it. Right now, all I want is time to accept what's happened." Splaying her hands across her stomach, her voice dropped to a whisper. "Regardless of what Travis decides, this baby is wanted and will be loved."

"Of course he will," Suzanne huffed out.

A small grin broke across Isabella's face. "You think it will be a boy?"

"I hope so. Newt needs a town boy to play with."

"What about Emma?" Lena asked.

"There are plenty of girls in town. Not many boys."

"What about Caleb's son, Isaac?"

"He's five, Lena. Newt is two and a half."

Isabella and Carrie listened to them bantering back and forth, the exchange lightening the mood.

"Well, no one's going to know if I'm carrying a boy or girl for another five months. We'll discuss playmates then." Shoving up, Isabella walked to the kitchen. "Coffee?"

Lena and Suzanne nodded while Carrie walked to the door. "I need to get to the clinic and speak with Doc Worthington. I'll also talk to Griff about coming by, Isabella. Please don't worry. Travis is a good man. He'll make the right decision."

Placing both hands on her stomach, Isabella prayed her friend was right.

Chapter Ten

Carrie sat in Griffin's office, relaying Isabella's message to him and Francesca. Neither interrupted while she explained the situation. Both were stunned at Travis leaving.

"Under the circumstances, you might want to meet with her, Frannie."

Tapping fingers on her desk, Francesca looked at Carrie. "What do you think?"

"She's fragile right now. I wonder if Isabella might hold herself together better if Griff goes."

Francesca understood. "A man rather than a woman?"

"I suppose. I'm sure either of you would be fine."

Griffin leaned back in his chair, steepling fingers under his chin. He was savoring the memory of him and Carrie at Rocky Basin, and her reaction to his kisses. It would be best if they stayed in town, around others. Having her alone was too much of a temptation.

"Griff, are you all right going?"

"I'm fine meeting with her." He looked at Carrie. "Did she say when would be best?"

"Tomorrow should be fine. I got the sense there was a slight amount of urgency to her request."

Francesca's mouth thinned. "Understandable. She tells her husband about the baby, and he leaves. My guess is what she requires from us will give her peace of mind whether Travis returns or not."

Walking to a nearby cabinet, Francesca withdrew a file, handing it to Griffin. "The work I've done for Isabella."

Reviewing the contents, his brows rose. "I had no idea."

"Most people don't know the extent of her wealth. Her late husband was well situated with property, stocks, and a sizable amount of cash. She lives modestly, so most of what came to her upon his death is intact."

Griffin continued to review the documents. "From what Carrie told us, I'll be focusing on protecting the inheritance for her child."

Believing she'd done what had been promised, Carrie stood, her gaze on Griffin. "I should return to the clinic. Do you want me to let Isabella know you'll meet with her tomorrow?"

Setting the file aside, he joined her at the door. "I'll have Damon deliver a message to her this afternoon. I'll walk Carrie out, and return so we can discuss Isabella in more detail."

Instead of walking downstairs ahead of her, Griffin took her hand, unwilling to go another minute without touching her. "Are you all right?"

"I'm so sad for Isabella, and angry at Travis. How could a husband leave as he did?"

Squeezing her hand, he led her to the front door and outside. Facing her, Griffin took her other hand. "Travis is a good man who's struggling with his decision on children.

He needs time. I don't believe he plans to stay away long, Carrie."

"I hope you're right. The look of desolation on Isabella's face broke my heart." Before she thought about her words, she blurted them out. "I want children." Feeling her face heat, she placed a hand over her mouth, closing her eyes. A moment passed before she dared look at Griffin. His lips twitched at the corners, eyes crinkled in humor. "Are you laughing at me, Griffin MacKenzie?"

"Absolutely not."

Crossing her arms, she lifted her chin. "You'd better not be."

"Definitely not laughing."

"Pretend I didn't say anything."

"Already forgotten. May I ask a question?"

"Go ahead."

"Do you plan to marry and have children?" She was silent so long he lifted her chin to look in her eyes. "Carrie?"

Pursing her lips, she glanced away before answering. "Yes. Someday, I want to marry and have a family."

"Good, because I want the same." Glancing around, he decided not to act on his impulse to kiss her.

"Oh." Mischief glowed in her eyes. "Do you have someone in mind?"

"Yes, ma'am, I do. The woman is standing right in front of me."

"Is she?" A broad smile brightened her face as her heart pounded against her ribs.

"Have supper with me tonight."

"All right."

"I'll come by at five. We'll go to Eagle's Nest. I want to kiss you, but..."

Carrie lowered her voice. "Don't you dare. Gladys Poe is coming our way. I've heard she loves spreading gossip."

"Then I'll behave. For now. No promises about later."

She stepped away as the older woman, eyes narrowed on them, passed by. "Good morning, Mrs. Poe."

Stopping, she glanced between them, pinning Griffin with a sharp glare. "I heard a rumor you were courting Miss Galloway."

"It isn't a rumor if it's true, Mrs. Poe."

Sniffing, she shifted, balancing her sizable girth on both feet. "See that you do nothing to embarrass yourself, Miss Galloway. People aren't inclined to forgive breaches of propriety."

Carrie bit her lower lip, controlling the urge to laugh. "So true, Mrs. Poe. I'll be careful."

"I'll be moving on. Good day to both of you."

Griffin touched the brim of his hat. "Good day, ma'am."

When out of earshot, Carrie met his expectant gaze. "I'll see you this evening, Mr. MacKenzie."

"Already looking forward to it, Miss Galloway."

Watching her walk away, Griffin felt a sense of peace, as well as a prickle of fear. They'd settled something very important with few words. If all went as he hoped, Carrie would hold a major place in his future.

Dirty Dave dropped to his knees, burying his head in both hands. Sending up a prayer, he thanked God for his good fortune. The days in the territorial capital had allowed him to recover his strength, take care of his horse, and fill his pockets with men foolish enough to challenge him at cards.

"Yessiree bob. You certainly have blessed me." Bursting into laughter, he shoved himself up.

To think, a few years ago, he'd been a Baptist minister, full of righteous fire to spread God's word. His parents were proud of him, and the single women in the church flocked to him. He'd sampled the wares of those willing, ensuring them they'd done God's will. It was a miracle Dave's will matched his maker's.

Dave didn't know when it all went wrong. Maybe the blame could be placed on the two women who'd taken his assertions of love to heart. Such young, silly women.

When one announced she carried his child, he'd withdrawn the little money he had in the bank, packed up his few belongings, mounted Scarlett, and took off. But not before posting the following Sunday's sermon to the pulpit.

A few weeks later, out of money and starving, he began to regret his decision to ride out. He'd considered going back and marrying the girl. Rejecting the idea, he picked another profession. How hard could robbing banks be? Dave discovered it wasn't hard at all with three other men.

Opening a window, he poked his head outside. Across the street, Scarlett drank from a trough in the stables. "About time we got out of here, old girl."

As if she'd heard him, the horse raised her head and whinnied.

"Tomorrow morning, Scarlett."

Closing the window, Dave made a sweep of the room. Not much to pack. A new shirt and pants. He wanted a new hat, the one he'd wear into Splendor. Brown, with a wide brim to hide his face. And a heavy coat to replace the one he'd lost between Moosejaw and Big Pine. Moving between the hotel, saloon, and nearby restaurant didn't require one. Now, he did.

Dave had learned a lot about Splendor from the men around the card table, bartender, and waitress where he took his meals.

The same as Sheriff Parker Sterling in Big Pine, no one wanted to go against Gabe Evans and his deputies in Splendor. Most had fought in the war, many were former Texas Rangers. All were dead shots with a gun.

Dave wasn't going after the sheriff or his men. His target had been a lawman once, a long time ago in Texas. He'd been told a pen and a quick mind were now the man's weapons of choice. All the better for Dave. An unarmed man made an easy target, the same as the cities back east who wouldn't allow civilians to carry firearms.

A prickle at the back of his neck caused Dave to again look out the window. There was just enough daylight left to recognize a tall man wearing a brown hat. On the street below, Sheriff Sterling stopped in front of the hotel. With him were two deputies. They spoke for a few minutes before walking inside.

They could be here for anything, though it wouldn't take three men for a friendly talk. Dave knew their presence held a purpose.

Pulling the saddlebags from under the bed, he stuffed his few belongings inside, including the new shirt and pants. A new hat would have to wait, as would a heavy coat.

Strapping on his gunbelt, he checked the chambers of the six-shooter. Satisfied, he shoved the weapon into its holster before sliding a knife to a sheath and securing it to his belt.

Last, he lifted the mattress, gripping a pouch filled with his winnings. Slipping it into the saddlebags, he slung them over his shoulder before picking up his rifle. Recently cleaned, he knew it was loaded and ready.

Checking outside once more, he exited his room, taking the back stairs. He knew they ended at a door leading to the narrow passageway between the hotel and the shop next door.

Going right would lead him to the main street. Left would take him to a back street. Using the darkening sky, Dave could weave his way between buildings without being seen.

It took longer than expected to reach the stables. Sterling had dispatched more deputies to watch the back street. Waiting until they disappeared into nearby businesses, he kept going until he slipped through the back gate of the stables.

His saddle, blanket, and tack hung a few feet from Scarlett. Five minutes was all he needed before mounting.

A few bills in his hand, he tugged an old nail from the wall separating one stall from another. Holding up the money, he shoved the nail back into the original hole.

Satisfied, he swung into the saddle. Bending at the waist, he reined Scarlett through the back gate and away from the hotel across the street.

Careful not to draw attention, Dave entered the main street, and headed west. He could see the end of town. Riding past the last buildings, he kept the slow, easy pace for another hundred yards.

He didn't breathe easy until Big Pine was a tiny dot in the distance.

Chapter Eleven

Splendor

Thomas slipped between tables at the Eagle's Nest, Carrie and Griffin following. "Will this suit you, Mr. MacKenzie?" The table for two, situated in a quiet corner of the dining room, had been adorned with candles and a vase filled with dried flowers.

"It's fine, Thomas. Thank you." Moving behind Carrie's chair, he pulled it out.

"Thank you, Griff."

Handing them a list of items for the evening, Thomas took their order for a bottle of red wine, leaving the couple alone.

Carrie glanced around with appreciation. "The restaurant is so beautiful in the evening. Everything sparkles."

Griffin smiled, thinking the most beautiful sight was Carrie. The blue dress highlighted her auburn hair, brightening her sapphire blue eyes.

"Yes, it does."

Switching her attention to him, she discovered his gaze locked on her. Breath hitching, she relaxed at the sight of Thomas approaching with a bottle of wine and two glasses.

Opening the bottle, he poured a portion for Griffin, waiting for his nod before filling both their glasses. "I'll give you time to make decisions."

"Thank you, Thomas." Lifting his glass, Griffin tipped it out toward Carrie. "To a wonderful evening."

Touching her glass to his, she took a sip. "Oh, my. It's delicious."

"Have you never had wine here?"

"The one time I came for supper, everyone drank coffee. We did have sherry with our dessert." She tapped her glass. "This is much better."

Griffin couldn't take his gaze from hers. Beautiful, smart, funny, and fun. She brought light to a man whose life had included little of it. Carrie was perfect, more than he deserved. How could he tell her about the dark periods of his life, the people he'd killed? Could he risk losing her because of his ugly past?

Thomas appeared to take their orders. Answering Carrie's questions, he poured a little more wine into their glasses before turning toward the kitchen.

"Do you plan to stay in Splendor?"

Griffin cocked his head, surprised at her question. "Yes. The partnership with Frannie is going well, my friends have established their ranch, and I plan to buy land in Rocky Basin. I want to put down roots, Carrie." He didn't mention marrying and having children, thinking he'd already stated his intentions earlier.

"The MacLarens seem to be fine people. I've never been to their ranch."

"I'll take you there. Sunday, if you're free." Before then, he'd speak with Bram, his wife, Selina, or Thane, letting them know to expect visitors. "Will you allow me to escort you to church?"

"I'd love to sit with you, Griff."

Scooting his chair closer, he reached out to cover her hand with his. "I've traveled across this entire country, worked at a variety of jobs, met some interesting people. No place has mattered as much as Splendor. The people have faced blizzards, gunslingers, kidnappers, rustlers, and earthquakes. They genuinely care about each other. It's rare to see such unity."

Sipping her wine, she thought of his words and how few places she'd been. "I've lived in New York and here. Until learning about Splendor from Rachel Pelletier, I thought New York offered all I'd ever want. Her letters made Montana and the town sound almost magical." A small grin appeared. "I'm certain that sounds strange."

"Not at all."

"Her descriptions of people and the territory were so vivid, bringing the town to life in my mind. When she encouraged a group of us to travel across country, I first thought she was becoming feeble-minded. Rachel continued to write letters, some with pictures she'd drawn of the ranch, the town. One was of a Blackfoot village. Receiving her letters felt almost the same as Christmas." Taking another sip of wine, she glanced around the restaurant, smiling at people she recognized.

"Francesca was the first to make the decision to leave. Amelia Newhall was next. I agreed soon afterward, as did Rose Keenan."

"And Georgina?"

"She was the last. The rest of us had told our families, purchased tickets, and were packing when she decided to join us. I saw a great many places from my seat on the train, but rarely stepped outside to visit the towns. If I were to do it again, I'd take my time."

Thomas arrived, halting the conversation to set plates before them. "May I get you anything else?"

After a quick glance at Carrie, Griffin answered. "We're fine for now, Thomas."

They spoke little for the first few minutes of eating, each savoring the steaks ordered. After several bites, Carrie spoke.

"Rachel told me most of the beef is from the Pelletier ranch. Some is purchased from Dom Lucero. Wherever this is from, it's excellent."

"So is mine." Griffin scooped up boiled potatoes. "Do you plan to stay in Splendor?"

"I do. Georgina is talking about going on to San Francisco."

His fork stilled for a moment before stabbing a piece of steak. "You have no interest in accompanying her?"

"None. At least, not right now." She held his gaze a moment longer than needed before focusing on her meal.

Griffin tucked Carrie close, threading his fingers through hers as they walked along the boardwalk. Their conversation made it obvious both wanted the same kind of future. The question remained whether they wanted it with each other.

They walked as far as the boardinghouse before facing the street. The last few days of sun had melted much of the snow in town, creating a muddy slush. Bending, he scooped Carrie into his arms.

Laughing, she wrapped her arms around his neck. "What are you doing?"

"Making sure you don't ruin your dress."

"You know I'm wearing boots. I did cross to the Eagle's Nest without soiling my clothes."

"All right. I confess it was an excuse."

Her brows drew together. "An excuse?"

"To hold you close."

Reaching the other side, he took his time setting her down. Carrie's hands lingered on his shoulders before sliding them down his arms, her gaze meeting his.

"I want to kiss you, Carrie."

"Yes."

He glanced around, noting the empty boardwalk and street. Lowering his head, his mouth covered hers. Wrapping his arms around her, he deepened the kiss. He took his time, hearing Carrie's moan.

Not wanting to stop, knowing he had no choice, Griffin lifted his head. Her eyes were closed. When she opened them, he saw desire clear in her gaze. Kissing her once more, he stepped away.

"I should get you home."

Slipping her arm through his, Griffin led them along the boardwalk. He kept the pace slow, wanting to keep her close as long as possible.

His thoughts lingered on when to tell Carrie about his past. How to relate all he'd done without her turning away in disgust.

Sunday, he'd escort her to church, then to the MacLarens'. She'd enjoy getting away from town to visit with Selina. Griffin doubted the women knew each other well. All the more reason to make the trip to the ranch south of town.

Carrying her across another street, he didn't set Carrie down until stopping at her front door. His movements were even slower this time, holding her against him much longer than required. He might have held her for hours if the door hadn't opened. Georgina stood with her arms crossed and a stern expression.

"Good evening, Georgina."

"Griffin. Do you intend to allow her inside?"

Glancing down at Carrie's flushed face, he smiled. "In a few more minutes. There is more I have to say." Waiting a moment, he pinned Georgina with a stern look. "A private conversation."

Dropping her arms, she shook her head while closing the door.

"I should go inside, Griff."

"And you will." The words he intended to say stuck in his throat.

A minute passed before Carrie touched his arm, head tilting toward him. "Do you intend to say it tonight?"

Jaw tight, mouth drawn in a thin line, he cleared his throat. "Yes, tonight." Seconds ticked by, Carrie staring up at him.

"Well?"

Removing his hat, Griffin ran fingers through his hair before setting the hat back in place. "You know I care about you, Carrie."

"I have gotten that impression. And I care about you."

"What you don't know is to what degree." Swallowing the fear at admitting what he'd never said to another woman, he laced the fingers of one hand with hers. "I've never felt the depth of feelings for any woman I do for you. You're on my mind when falling asleep, and when waking in the morning. An inordinate amount of each day is spent thinking about you."

Seeing the twinkle in her eyes, the expectant expression, he cleared his throat. "We haven't known each other long, so this may seem premature. What I'm trying to say is I want you in my life. Not for a few weeks or months, but for much longer. I know it's too soon to talk marriage, however, you deserve to know my emotions concerning you run quite deep."

Blinking, letting out the breath she'd been holding, Carrie tightened her fingers around his. "Well, you are quite the surprise, Mr. MacKenzie."

"I am?"

"Some men never express what you've admitted, not even after being married for years. You, however, are quite eloquent. You should know, the depth of my feelings also run deep. Extremely deep, in fact." A slow grin spread across her face. "It's quite freeing to get it out, don't you think?"

Throat thick, he gave a crisp nod.

Placing a hand on his chest, her grin began to fade. "Are you already regretting what you said?"

"No. Not at all." He ran a hand down her arm, searching his mind for the right words. "There is more. My past..." Glancing away, he tried again. "I've done things which may make you change your mind about me."

"Things you regret?"

"I don't regret any of my actions. However, you may not choose to be with me once you understand all I've done."

Dropping her hand, she squared her shoulders. "Then I suppose you should tell me so I can decide for myself."

Knowing the history he was about to admit might mean tonight would be their last time together, he met her unwavering gaze. Before he could speak, a bullet flew past them, lodging in the column of the porch. Taking her arm, he kicked open the front door, shoving her inside.

"Extinguish the lamp and stay down." When Georgina's door opened, he shouted the same warning. The door slamming shut gave him her answer. "Get into your bedroom, Carrie. Hide away from the window and wait for me."

It was then Carrie saw the gun in his hand. "Griff…"

"Just do as I say." Without another word, he slipped out the back door.

Chapter Twelve

"He must've run off right after taking the shot, Gabe." Griffin paced inside the jail, running a hand through his hair for a second time. "One shot and gone is the way I see it."

"A warning." Gabe sat at his desk, Hex Boudreaux across from him. Both had heard the shot and came running.

Hex rubbed the back of his neck. "Men don't warn people much around here. They shoot to kill. I'm thinking he flat missed his target."

"Meaning me?" Griff blew out a low curse.

Shrugging, Hex thought of the two women in the house. "Unless you believe someone would be gunning for Carrie or Georgina."

"No. I'm the target." Which meant being in their presence put the women in danger. Griff didn't care for the direction of his thoughts.

A pained expression pinched Gabe's face. "You might want to stay away from Carrie until we arrest who's after you."

Chest squeezing, Griff knew keeping a good distance from Carrie would be the smart decision. He'd seen the consequences of stray bullets plowing into innocents, leaving them injured or dead. It would devastate him if she got caught in the crosshairs of a gunfight. He knew no other way to protect her than put a hold on their courting until he hunted down and killed whoever gunned for him.

"Unless I find him first," Griff muttered.

Gabe leaned forward, his jaw set. "Listen to me. You aren't a Range Detective any longer. Keep your six-shooter in its holster and let me and my deputies find him. It'd be even better if you stored it in your desk." They both knew the last would never happen.

Unable to lie to a man who'd become a friend, Griff's hard glare met Gabe's. "I'll make no promises. If someone bushwhacks or draws on me, I'm going to shoot back. My gun is staying right where it is." His hand rested on the handle of the six-shooter.

Reaching into his desk, Gabe pulled out a sheet of paper and pencil, sliding them toward Griff. "List who might be after you. Men you've sent to jail, people you killed who might have relatives searching for you, anyone with a grudge. I'll see if I can match anyone on your list to what's in the stack of wanted posters."

Griff waved off the paper and pencil. "I'll think on it and get you a list tomorrow."

Pulling out his pocket watch, he figured there was still time to stop by Carrie's on his way home. It would be a short visit to make certain she and Georgina were all right. He hadn't made up his mind about telling her tonight or tomorrow about not seeing each other for a while.

Scraping the legs of his chair over the rough wood floor, Griff stood. "I'd better get going."

Gabe rose along with him. "Remember what I said."

"What was it?" Chuckling at Gabe's frustrated expression, Griff stopped at the door. "I'm not going to shoot someone in the back, Sheriff. You can count on that."

Griff didn't notice Gabe motioning at Hex to follow him home.

Griff took a different route than usual, passing in front of Ruby's Palace, cutting between the meat market and bookstore to skirt the side of Hawke's house. Hex followed a couple dozen paces behind. Stopping at his street, he waited for Hex to catch up.

"You see anything?"

The deputy grimaced as his gaze continued to scan the area in front and behind them. "No. Whoever shot at you is gone. At least for tonight."

The two stared across the street at the house Carrie and Georgina rented from Noah Brandt, the owner of the livery, stables, tack shop, and many of the houses in Splendor. Griff and Hex also rented from him.

"What are you going to do?"

Griff turned toward Hex. "Determine who shot at me, find him, and deliver him to the jail."

"If he fires on you?"

His mouth twisted into a feral grin. "Then Gabe will get a body."

Hex's jaw worked as he considered his next words. "I'll help you. You can count Zeke in, also. How are your tracking skills?"

"Average at best."

"Cash Coulter, Beau Davis, and Travis Dixon are the best around. I heard Travis is staying at the Pelletier ranch. Word is Isabella is with child."

Griff thought of the meeting arranged with Isabella the following day. "A messy business. I wouldn't turn down help from Cash and Beau."

"I'll talk to them." Adjusting his hat, Hex clasped Griff's shoulder before walking the short distance to his house.

Griff found himself envying the deputy. When Hex stepped inside, the man would be welcomed by his wife, her sister, and his daughter.

He needed to stop delaying the inevitable and speak with Carrie while a light still glowed through the windows. A chance still existed the shot was wild, not meant for either him or Carrie. Griff didn't believe it. He'd made enemies, some he knew about. His instincts told him a perceived wrong from his past had caught up with him.

It had been a long time since he'd felt concern over the men he'd killed. They'd all been righteous deaths, no innocents among them.

Griff thought of the list Gabe requested. Three men came to mind, each one capable of tracking him across country to exact vengeance. Not one would feel guilt over killing innocents to destroy him.

There's nothing he wouldn't do to keep her safe, including letting her go. Would Carrie understand it wouldn't be for long? Or would she perceive his words as an excuse to pull away?

Griff also had to consider the fact he may not live much longer. The shooter had missed today. It didn't mean he'd miss again. Should he warn Carrie? The idea didn't sit well with him, as if he'd already conceded the shooter would win.

Forcing his feet to move, he crossed the street, hesitating a moment before knocking. The door opened within seconds. The relief on Carrie's face weighed heavy on him. He never wanted to cause her worry.

Opening the door wider, she motioned him inside before wrapping her arms around his waist. "You're all right."

Holding her, he rested his chin on the top of her head. "I'm fine, sweetheart."

A long moment passed before she dropped her arms, stepping out of his embrace. "I couldn't sleep without knowing. There's coffee."

Ignoring the offer, he took her hand, leading them to the sofa. "We should talk."

"All right." Something in his voice warned her to prepare for bad news.

He continued to hold her hand for several minutes as he considered his words. Exhaling a long breath, he searched her face.

"There are men from my past, Carrie. Men who wouldn't regret my death."

"I don't understand."

"You see me as an attorney, which I am. What you don't know is the life I led before moving to California and meeting the MacLarens."

Squeezing his hand, she encouraged him to continue. "Tell me, Griff."

"My last job was as a Range Detective for the Cattle Raisers Association in Texas. It involved tracking down rustlers and bringing them in for trial. A few gave themselves up. Most didn't. I was involved in a shootout in Finn's Saloon a few weeks ago."

"Yes, I heard about it."

"The men were part of a gang in Texas I helped eliminate."

She stared down at their joined hands. "Did they follow you all the way to Montana?"

"I don't think so. The leaders of the gang appeared shocked to see me. Not what you'd expect from men hunting someone. They went to trial and are now residents of the prison near Deer Lodge."

"What about the shot tonight? Do you believe it came from a member of their gang?"

"Maybe. Not real probable. My guess is any of the outlaws who were in the saloon that day would be a couple hundred miles away by now. Makes more sense it's a different threat. Could be one man, or there could be more."

"Perhaps it was a random shot, Griff."

"It wasn't random, Carrie." His thumb made circles on the back of her hand. He didn't know if the gesture was to soothe him or her.

They sat in silence for several minutes, the tension between them growing as each second passed. Griff's throat thickened, knowing what he said next would change their budding relationship.

"You and I can't be seen together for a while, Carrie."

Her body stilled for a moment as she took in his words. "You're calling off our courtship."

"It's not what I want, but keeping you safe is my main priority. Being seen with me is too dangerous until whoever fired at me is caught."

She pulled her hand from his, her voice turning flat. "But you have no idea who did the shooting or how long it will take to find them?"

"No."

"I see." Scooting away, she stood. "Are you sure you don't want coffee?"

Shaking his head, he studied her. The joy of earlier in the evening had disappeared, replaced by a stoic resolve. She'd accept his decision without complaint or argument.

"Doing what's right isn't always easy, is it?"

Griff continued to watch her, uneasy with the quick acceptance of their situation. "No."

"And you're certain this is the only way to proceed?"

Right now, he wasn't sure of anything. "First, I know the bullet was meant for me. Whoever pulled the trigger wouldn't have cared if it hit you. Innocents are people who get in their way, nothing more. I'd never be able to live with myself if anything happened to you."

"So I'm to act as if there was never anything between us."

"For a while."

"Which tells me nothing."

Rising, he closed the distance between them, reaching out to place a hand on her shoulder. "My hope is we'll track down the person soon. There are few places to hide, and strangers stand out in Splendor. Gabe may agree to let Cash and Beau help me and Hex track the shooter." Sliding the hand on her shoulder to the back of her neck, he drew her to his chest. "This isn't what I want, Carrie. You must know that."

Resting her head on his chest, she quelched the urge to wrap her arms around his waist.

"If you don't want to wait, I'll understand."

Stiffening, she pulled back. "What are you saying?"

"Well, if you become interested in someone else—" He got no further before Carrie interrupted.

"Don't be ridiculous, Griffin MacKenzie. I'll wait as long as it takes. Don't assume you can get rid of me so easily." Jutting her chin out, she dared him to argue.

The knot of worry in his chest began to ease as a slow grin appeared on his face. Staring down onto her beautiful face, he lowered his head, his mouth covering hers.

Chapter Thirteen

Griff stood behind an overstuffed chair in Isabella's living room, noting how the grim expression on her face matched his mood. The melancholy plaguing him since leaving Carrie's the night before continued to vex him.

She'd taken the news of not seeing each other better than he'd expected. Better than him, if he were being honest. He already missed her.

"Thank you for coming, Griff."

The distress in Isabella's voice drew him back to the reason for his visit. "Of course. Miss Galloway explained you want to modify the provisions in your will. Are you still familiar with the contents?"

"I am. It's quite simple. If anything happens to me, everything goes to my husband, Travis." Staring down at the clasped hands in her lap, she let out a shaky breath. "Are you aware I'm with child?"

"Yes, ma'am, I am."

"And that Travis left me because of the baby?"

Griff gave a slight nod. "He's staying at the Pelletier ranch, correct?"

"As far as I know. It's been three days and I haven't heard anything from him."

"Do you believe he won't return, Isabella?"

Face clouding, she didn't respond right away. Instead, she stood. "Would you care for coffee?"

"If it isn't too much trouble."

"No trouble at all."

He watched as she went through the motions of preparing coffee, setting the pot on the stove. Griff wouldn't rush her. The woman faced tough decisions, and a possible future without her husband. A man Griff knew Isabella loved without reservation. Through it all, her thoughts were on the baby growing inside her.

"Here you are."

Taking the cup she offered, he waited until she sat down to take his seat. Taking a sip, he grinned. "This coffee is excellent."

"Thank you. Gabe makes sure I get part of each shipment from New York. He knows how much Travis..." She hesitated a moment, as if weighing her words. "And I love it. I do have milk and sugar."

"Black is fine."

Setting her cup down, she sat forward on the chair. "My intention is to protect my baby. If Travis doesn't return, and something happens to me, a guardian must be named and suitable financial arrangements."

"Have you settled on a guardian?"

"Lena and Gabe. I've discussed it with her and she'd spoken with Gabe. They're both agreeable. Although, I do believe Gabe will try to beat some sense into Travis if he doesn't return soon."

Griff suppressed a chuckle. He expected nothing less from the respected lawman. "I might join him." A small smile appeared on her face, which was his intent. "I'll make sure they are listed as guardians in the event of your death.”

“Or incapacity to make sound decisions for my child.”

“Let me speak with Frannie about the appropriate wording to avoid guardianship transferring if any incapacity is temporary.”

“Thank you, Griff.”

“As for financial changes, what are your wishes?”

“Please understand, Travis has been a wonderful husband and provider. He’s such a hard worker, and you’ll never meet a more honorable man.” Noticing the slight doubt on Griff’s face, she explained. “I agreed to no children when we married. Although the baby was as much a surprise to me as Travis, he sees it as a betrayal. My betrayal. Perhaps he’s right. No matter where the blame lies, there is a baby to look after. I want eighty percent of my estate to go to the child, with twenty percent going to Travis. The bullheaded man won’t take the money, but it’s to be in my will nonetheless.”

“You’re set on those percentages?”

“I am. If he won’t accept the money, it will continue in his name for when he’s no longer able to work. The man has a horrible inability to look to his future. We’ve discussed it many times, always with the same outcome. He simply refuses to look beyond today.” She shrugged. “It’s his way. Is there anything else you need from me to make the changes?”

“If there is, I’ll be back to discuss it with you.”

"Fair enough, Griff. How soon may the changes be made?"

"It depends on you. Three days isn't long, Isabella. Most men would consider a week or two about right for a major decision. I'd suggest making the changes, but perhaps holding off a few days before signing."

"I appreciate your concern, however, my wishes are to take care of this right away. If Travis does return, you and I will go through this one more time." Standing, she moved toward the door, signaling the end of their meeting. "If I might ask one more thing from you?"

"Name it."

"Would you have time to stop by the jail to let Gabe know I'm ready?"

Joining her at the door, he cocked his head to the side. "Ready?"

"He'll know what I mean." Drawing the door open, he saw the moment she began to sag under the weight of her decisions.

"I'll let Gabe know, and have the changes to you within a few days. Is there anything else I can do?"

"You've already eased my mind a great deal." When he stepped outside, she spoke again. "I do hope whatever is between you and Carrie works out. My sense is you two are meant to be together."

Isabella's last words haunted Griff for three long days—more than seventy-two hours without seeing Carrie. He believed what his client said was true. They belonged together. Once they found the shooter, he'd waste no time letting Carrie know.

Griff's days were divided between legal work and searching for the mysterious shooter. Hex, Zeke, Cash, and Beau helped when they could. There was little to go on. One shot at night. The snow had already been trampled by foot and horse traffic, leaving nothing for the expert trackers to find.

Another storm threatened the area. The snow had begun falling late the night before, already piling another foot on the ground.

Enoch Weaver, a former lawyer who spent his days bundled up on a bench outside the jail, predicted two more feet before the storm passed. Hex had spoken to Enoch about watching for anyone new to town who had the look of a gunslinger. Not much to go on, but the older man had been known to be quite astute at recognizing danger.

Griff set the last of the documents on the stack at the corner of his desk. Among them was Isabella's revised last will and testament. He'd heard nothing of Travis returning, which bothered Griff a great deal.

Isabella had moved in with Gabe and Lena. He knew the two women were as close as sisters. The change would be good for both women, and provide support for Isabella if Travis didn't change his mind and come home.

Griff knocked, then stepped into his partner's office. "I'm leaving, Frannie. Is Zeke walking you home?"

"He should be here soon. Be careful, Griff. Maybe you should wait for Zeke and me."

"I appreciate your concern, but I'll be careful." He didn't mention putting her in danger wasn't going to happen. "See you in the morning."

The stairs to the first floor gave him time to decide whether to stop at McCall's for supper or fix something at home. The decision was easy since there was nothing at his place to eat. Buttoning his coat, placing a hand on his hat, he stepped outside into winds gusting in all directions.

He estimated the snow had increased to two feet, making wagon travel difficult. Horses didn't fare any better. Without the covered boardwalk, even the short distance to McCall's would've been difficult.

Heat slammed into him when he pushed the door open, the aromas of Elmer's cooking wafting through the dining room. Betts and her husband, Ernie, had bought the restaurant several years earlier, earning a reputation for good food and large portions.

"Griffin. It's good to see you." Betts approached, a cup of coffee already in her hand. "Not many are braving the storm tonight. Sit wherever you want."

Shrugging out of his coat, he picked a table, taking the offered cup from Betts' hand. "What's the special tonight?"

"Meatloaf, applesauce, and mashed potatoes."

"Sounds good. Thanks." He sipped the coffee, spotting a used Big Pine newspaper on the chair of a nearby table.

The headlines were months old. Three caught his attention. The first discussed the establishment of Yellowstone Park in Wyoming several months earlier. A shorter article presented the pros and cons of Montana becoming a state.

The last, brief story stole his attention. A Colorado sheriff had organized a search of buildings in Denver. The man they sought was identified as Dirty Dave Dugan, an outlaw wanted for numerous offenses, including killing a woman during a shootout in Denver. Mrs. Hardin, wife of Judge Hoodoo Hardin, had been killed when a stray bullet pierced her chest. Dugan had escaped, witnesses claiming he headed north.

"Dirty Dave Dugan," Griff whispered, the name tasted bitter on his tongue.

"Tonight's special." Betts set a plate in front of him. "More coffee?" When he continued to stare at the newspaper, she tried again. "Griff?"

The sharp tone jarred him from the article. "Sorry."

"Coffee?"

He held up his cup. "Please."

She glanced at the paper, then back at him. "Let me know if you want seconds."

Instead of answering, his gaze landed back on the story, a ball of anger lodging in his chest. Could Dirty Dave have found him in Splendor? Was he the one who'd shot at him?

Griff thought of an afternoon in a rowdy Texas town years earlier. The Range Detective badge identified him as a lawman tasked with locating and arresting rustlers. Griff had never been comfortable believing he enforced the law. The ranchers had hired him because of his skills with a gun, not his legal proficiency.

Dirty Dave and another man had emerged from the bank, each carrying a bag in one hand, and gripping a gun in the other. Handkerchiefs covered their faces.

Griff had finished his business, eaten lunch, and looked forward to a bath and game of cards before returning to his room in a local boardinghouse. The appearance of the two outlaws caught him by surprise, but hadn't slowed his reaction.

Drawing his gun, he'd shouted for the two to drop their guns and raise their hands. The shorter of the two fired at Griff, who'd gotten off two shots before ducking into an open door. One of his bullets had found its mark.

Reaching out as he'd fallen toward his partner, the outlaw had gripped the man's handkerchief, dragging it down his face as he'd gritted out, "Help me, Dave."

Grasping the man's collar, Dave had attempted to drag him toward their horses, letting go when Griff's bullets whizzed past his face. Swinging into his saddle, Dave had fired over his shoulder while spurring his horse out of town. The local sheriff had identified the dead outlaw as Dave's brother.

Thinking back on it now, Griff recalled the local sheriff identifying the dead man as Bob Dugan, Dave's younger brother. He hadn't thought much about possible consequences at the time. Revenge now sat hard in his gut.

Finishing his meal, he placed money on the table and waved at Betts. The storm had gotten worse in the short time he'd been in McCall's. Tugging up his collar, Griff fought his way against the gusting wind to the jail.

Snow had drifted to a foot high against the jail door, indicating no one had entered or left in a while. Shoving the door open, he first saw the empty desk, indicating Gabe had already left for home. Shifting, he spotted a lone figure at the stove, watching him.

"Shane."

"Evening, Griff. I hear you have some trouble."

"I may have figured out who took the shot at me and Carrie."

Shane's body stiffened at the name of the woman he'd once considered courting. "I hadn't heard about Carrie being with you. Is she all right?"

"Fine. I'm keeping my distance from her until the shooter is arrested."

"Yeah, I heard you were courting her. She's a real fine lady."

"Do you mind if I go through the wanted posters?"

Shrugging, Shane set down the cup to pull open a drawer and reach inside. He dropped the stack in the center of the desk.

"Tell me who you're looking for and I'll help."

Splitting the stack, Griff sat down. "Dirty Dave Dugan."

An odd expression appeared on Shane's face. Opening the desk's center drawer, he lifted the latest telegrams. Sorting through them, he stopped on one. "Dirty Dave Dugan, right?" He slid the telegram toward Griff.

It was from Sheriff Parker Sterling alerting Gabe to an outlaw believed to be on his way to Splendor.

Dirty Dave Dugan.

Chapter Fourteen

Judge Hoodoo Hardin entered the eastern boundary of Moosejaw, face a mask of ice from the recent storm. Lifting a gloved hand, he attempted to stroke his handlebar mustache, finding it frozen stiff. Realizing one twist and it could break, he dropped his hand to grip the saddlehorn.

Mid-morning, and the small town bustled with activity, a crowd hovering out front of the bank. Closing the distance, he reined up a couple businesses down, his gaze not moving from the growing mass of people. Curiosity warred against his desire for a whiskey and food, curiosity winning.

Lowering his heavy weight to the ground, he grunted at the feel of boots on ice. At five-feet-seven, he wasn't a tall man, yet Hoodoo's presence demanded attention. This didn't change in Moosejaw.

Face set, he ambled toward the front of the bank, the crowd parting without him saying a word. A deputy stood watch at the front door, a human shield, his intense, dark eyes locking on Hoodoo's. The man's stiffening posture made it clear the judge wasn't welcome.

"Where's the sheriff?"

"Inside, but he's left orders no one is to enter."

Unable to see around the deputy, he pulled himself up to get a glimpse over the man's shoulder. An average-sized, lean man wearing a badge spoke with another in a rumpled suit. He guessed them to be the bank manager and sheriff. The two stared down at a small man on the floor, his movements limited by a bulky pair of handcuffs.

"You tell your sheriff Judge Hoodoo Hardin wants to enter."

A smirk twisted the deputy's face. "It won't help."

"Tell him. *Now*, Deputy." The command in his voice drew the attention of those inside and outside the bank.

"What's the ruckus?"

"Sorry, Sheriff, but this man—"

"That you, Hoodoo?" Moving past the deputy, a smile appeared. "Darn if it isn't."

"How are you, John?" He accepted the sheriff's outstretched hand.

"It appears I'm a good sight better than you. Come inside where it's warm."

Shaking what he could of the lingering snow from his clothes, Hoodoo walked straight toward the handcuffed man on the ground. Studying the culprit, he leaned closer, noting a face with clear skin, a pert nose, and angry blue eyes. Long wisps of blonde hair stuck to the face.

"This woman do something, John?"

"What woman?"

Moving aside, Hoodoo nodded toward what he was certain would turn out to be a female, not a male. Kneeling, John pushed his hat back, studying her the same as Hoodoo.

"I'll be darn. Guess it doesn't change anything. She was still part of a group who robbed the bank." Pulling off her hat, blonde hair slipped out from a loose bun. "Son of a gun." Reaching out, he helped her to stand. "What's your name?"

Piercing blue eyes met his before she turned away, not answering.

"Who was riding with you?"

Body going rigid, her mouth pulled into a tight line.

Motioning for the second of his two deputies, John dragged the young woman forward. "Get her to the jail." Hands on hips, he watched the young man escort the woman outside. "And get her something to eat."

"A woman. Can you believe it, Hoodoo?"

"Happening more and more." Glancing around the bank, he noticed the manager a few feet away. "How many robbers were there?"

"Four. The one arrested was the smallest, and most restless of them." Removing his spectacles, he pulled a cloth from his pocket, cleaning the glass with shaky hands. Still trembling, he set them back in place. "First time we've had a robbery since I've been in Moosejaw."

"Anything in particular you noticed about the other three?" Hoodoo watched the manager pale at the question.

"No, sir. My attention was on the big guns each held."

John looked at the teller, who'd remained quiet since the robbery. "Could the other three have been women?"

Sitting in a chair, hands clenched in his lap, he shook his head. "Sorry, Sheriff. They looked like men to me. But who could tell with them wearing handkerchiefs?"

John's attention returned to the manager. "Are you planning to close for the day?"

"Oh, no. People will think we're out of money. I planned to make an announcement to those outside. Probably place a note on the door when we leave for lunch."

"Might be a good idea to close for lunch now, give yourself time to settle down before seeing customers." John pivoted to look at Hoodoo. "Let's get something to eat, and you can tell me why you're so far north."

Splendor

Gabe held up the latest telegram from Big Pine sheriff, Parker Sterling, features grim. "No sign of Dave Dugan in Big Pine." Setting it down, he held up another. "The Moosejaw sheriff says he hasn't been spotted there, either. He did mention a bank robbery. They arrested one of the outlaws. A woman."

Griff's brows rose. "I'll be darned. Do you think they may have been the same four outlaws who robbed the bank here?"

Rubbing the stubble on his jaw, Gabe shrugged. "Can't ignore the possibility. Four outlaws raided a bank in Big Pine not long after ours was robbed. I believe they're all connected." Shoving both telegrams in a drawer, he placed his muscled arms on the desk, leaning forward. "None of this has anything to do with Dave Dugan. It's been almost a week, right?"

"Seven days." Six since Griff had seen Carrie. "I'd almost believed the bullet was some kind of stray. Knowing Dugan may be riding this way changed my way of thinking. It was him, I'm certain of it."

"Not sure the timing works, Griff. He was seen in Big Pine not more than seven days ago."

"It's a five to six hour ride by horse. Seven by stagecoach. He could've made it with time to spare."

"If you're right, Dugan would've had to locate you and set up the shot. I don't know, but he's the one person who makes sense. We need to show the wanted poster around town to see if anyone recognizes him."

Griff's mouth twisted into a wry grin. "Start with the saloons."

Sitting back, Gabe steepled fingers under his chin. "What are your plans?"

"Simple. Find Dugan."

"You're a citizen, not a lawman, Griff. Stay out of this and let me and my men take care of Dugan."

"We've already had this discussion. You know I can't do that."

Mouth quirking up at one corner, Gabe reached into his desk, palming a shiny object. Taking one more hard look at his friend, he tossed the badge at Griff as Beau Davis and Cash Coulter joined them.

"Then I don't have a choice but to deputize you."

Shoving up, Griff ignored the badge and the two deputies. "I work alone."

"Not on this, you don't. Either take the badge or you'll be spending your days in one of my luxury rooms in the back."

Settling fisted hands on his hips, he glowered at all three men. "Not going to happen."

He didn't notice Gabe nodding at Cash and Beau as he turned to leave. Before reaching the door, the large men moved toward each other, blocking his path. For a split second, he considered throwing a punch at one of them, knowing it would end with him locked in a cell.

Whirling around, his features hardened into an expression most men would turn away from. Not Gabe. "Dammit. You're asking too much."

"I'm protecting you, Griff." Standing, Gabe leaned a hip against the edge of the desk. "What would happen if you spotted Dugan and he drew on you?"

"I'd shoot to kill."

"And if there weren't any witnesses to testify he drew first?"

Pausing, Griff rubbed a hand over his face.

"I'll tell you what would happen. My deputies would arrest you, and you'd stand trial."

"I'd be acquitted."

"Maybe. You'd also lose a lot of time away from your law practice...and from Carrie. Hell, she might even think you drew your gun first."

"That wouldn't happen."

"Are you a hundred percent sure?" When Griff continued to pin him with cold eyes, Gabe continued. "Now, what would happen if you were deputized?" Griff stayed silent. "Come on. You're a well-respected attorney who's represented men arrested for killing someone. In the cases I know about, your clients were innocent, and cleared by a jury. That's not always the case for innocent people. Deer Lodge has a good percentage of men who didn't do the crimes that led them to prison. So, if you wore a badge, what would happen?"

Griff blew out a low curse. "There'd be more doubt about me being guilty."

"Odds are you wouldn't spend a single night in this wonderful establishment. Which way would you place your bet?"

Jaw clenching, he reached out and scooped up the badge. Opening his coat, he pinned it to his shirt. "Satisfied?"

Heading toward the door, he dared Beau and Cash to stop him this time. Stomping into the frigid afternoon air, he thundered along the boardwalk, trying to come up with a good explanation for Francesca.

Unable to hide their amusement, Beau and Cash chuckled, watching through the window as Griff stormed down the boardwalk. Facing Gabe, their laughter died at their boss's serious expression.

He motioned toward the chair. "Sit down." Picking up the telegrams, he held one out to each of them. "Our shooter may or may not be Dugan."

Cash glanced up from the telegram. "Griff's convinced it is."

"Regardless, if you see Dugan, arrest him. There are plenty of charges to send him away for a long time."

Beau's brows rose as he read the telegram. "A woman?"

"That's what the sheriff in Moosejaw says. Makes me wonder about the gang of four who robbed the bank here in Splendor."

Cash handed his telegram to Beau. "Are you thinking it's the same gang?"

"They hit us, then Big Pine, and now Moosejaw. I think it's a fair assumption. My guess is they'll do their best to free the one in Moosejaw, and either ride west or south."

Beau set the telegram down. "They wouldn't be stupid enough to hit us again."

Gabe stared past his deputies to the increasing storm outside. "Most who make their living as outlaws aren't all that smart."

Cash glanced at Beau, then Gabe. "What do you want us to do if they do return, and they're women?"

"If they fire at you, shoot to kill."

Chapter Fifteen

Dirty Dave Dugan studied the cards in his hand, gaze moving to the door every few seconds. Clean-shaven, hat low on his forehead, and wearing new clothes, no one would recognize him as the outlaw wanted in at least three states. The loss of his beloved mustache bothered him, but not as much as being discovered and arrested.

The small town intrigued him from the moment he'd arrived a week earlier. Other than the one mishap the first night, Dugan had laid low, biding his time. He saw no need to rush, the person he sought wouldn't be going anywhere.

"You gonna play or stare at your cards all day?"

Dave didn't doubt the deep, southern drawl was aimed at him. Looking up, his expression neutral, he eyed the older man dressed in what he considered gambling garb. A black suit, red brocade vest, slim silk tie, and a cheroot tucked lightly between his lips. Probably a dandy who'd frequented the Mississippi gambling boats. Taking no offense, Dave studied his cards once more.

"I'll hold."

Of the four men at the table, the dandy was the big loser. The other two kept even, betting little, folding more often than not, which they did with this hand.

Placing his cards on the table, the older man smirked, certain he'd won the hand. Without giving a hint of what he held, Dugan laid his cards down. The sound of a chair scraping across the scarred wood floor signaled there could be trouble. There were days a man could only lose so much. The dandy had reached his limit.

Before the older man could stand and draw, Dave had his gun pointed at the dandy's chest.

"You lost the hand fair and square. Either stay seated and play, or walk away." This came from the quietest of the other two men at the table.

Three sets of eyes focused on the dandy, waiting for his decision. After a tense moment, he stood, scooped up what was left of his money, and stalked off. The other two shared a look before both stood.

"Guess we'll be moseying off as well."

Dave picked up his whiskey and leaned back in his chair. Studying the amber liquid, he reflected on the deep, golden color before tossing it back. He appreciated an establishment offering pure whiskey, not the watered down stuff prevalent at most frontier saloons.

Tucking his winnings into a small, leather pouch, he headed to the bar. "What's the name of this place?"

"Dixie Saloon. You want another whiskey?" Amos Henderson's gaze moved over the man. As the original owner of the Wild Rose Saloon, he'd seen hundreds of gamblers come and go. Few made the hairs on his neck prickle, as did the man across the bar.

"Not now. Thanks."

Amos didn't move from his spot as the man walked out, turning right onto the boardwalk. Grabbing a rag, he wiped down the bar, his thoughts locked on the stranger.

He'd been in the saloon several times over the last week, always ordering one whiskey while playing cards. Nothing happened, which shouldn't bother Amos, yet his instincts warned him the man wasn't who he appeared.

Before he spoke with Gabe or one of the deputies, Amos made the decision to watch the man a few more days. If the unease continued, he'd head to the jail and voice his concern. Until then, he'd serve the man drinks, take his money, and hope his apprehension was unfounded.

Carrie finished with the last patient as the bell above the clinic door chimed. Taking a moment to clean the examination room, she stepped into the waiting area to find a tall, slender man in a stiff gray suit standing by the door. Doing a quick sweep of his body, seeing nothing to indicate an injury, she offered a welcoming smile.

"May I help you?"

A slow grin spread across his face as he stepped forward. "My name is Drake Ralston. I understand Clay McCord is a doctor here."

"Yes. Him and Doctor Worthington, although he's not here often. I'm Carrie Galloway, one of the nurses. Doctor McCord is upstairs. If you'd wait here, I'll get him for you."

Drake watched her bound up the stairs, his interest in the pretty nurse sparking. Letting out a breath, he closed his eyes, chastising himself for being attracted to another woman so soon after losing his wife. It had been two years since she succumbed to a fever, leaving him distraught and uncertain about his future. A letter from Clay a year earlier had drawn him out of his depressing existence.

"Drake. It is you!" In an uncharacteristic gesture, Clay pulled his friend into a quick hug. "I've thought about you often."

Emotion thick in his throat, Drake struggled to speak. "I hope I'm not interrupting your work."

"Not at all." Clay glanced behind him, spotting Carrie. "You've met Miss Galloway. Best nurse west of the Mississippi. Tell me what brings you to Splendor."

Fingering the hat in his hand, Drake lowered his voice, uncertain of how to proceed. "Shall I be frank?"

"Of course."

"You mentioned Doctor Worthington might be retiring, and I thought perhaps, if you haven't hired someone, well..."

Clay's eyes grew wide. "Are you interested?"

Clearing his throat, he nodded. "Yes. If you think I'd suit."

Turning to look at Carrie, he motioned her forward. "You've met Doctor Ralston."

"In a way. He didn't mention being a doctor."

"One of the best." Clay shifted back toward Drake. "Have you had supper?"

"Not yet."

"Excellent. You'll be coming home with me. My wife, Olivia, is a wonderful cook, and there's always plenty. Let me get my coat and hat."

Carrie slipped into her own coat, raising the collar to ward off the evening chill. "It was a pleasure meeting you, Doctor Ralston. With Clay's recommendation, I'm certain Doctor Worthington will want to speak with you." Lowering her voice, she leaned toward him. "He makes the final decisions, at least until he fully retires. I do hope you'll give Splendor a chance." Hearing footfalls on the stairs, she stepped away. "Good night, Doctors."

"Carrie, wait. Why don't you join us for supper? I know Olivia would love to see you."

Hesitating a moment, she shook her head. "Thank you for the invitation, but I have plans. Perhaps another time."

With a quick look at Drake, she rushed out into the already frigid evening. The sun had already set, leaving the three-quarter moon and a few oil lamps shining through windows to guide her home.

Her thoughts went to Griff, and the familiar sense of loss swept through her. A week had passed without his company. She missed the sound of his voice, his hearty laugh, and gracious nature. And his passionate kisses. Carrie also missed their shared lunches and suppers, the way he'd slip her arm through his as they strolled the boardwalk.

Feeling a cold ball of longing lodge in her chest, she forced herself not to watch for him. He'd been elusive since announcing his intention to stay away from her until he'd identified the threat against them. Thinking back on their conversation, she realized how naïve she'd been to believe Griff would dispatch the shooter within a few days.

"Miss Galloway."

The shout came from behind her, in a voice she recognized. Stopping, she waited for Morgan Wheeler to catch up. He touched the brim of his hat.

"Good evening, ma'am."

"Hello, Deputy."

"I'm on duty tonight. May I walk with you?"

Smiling up at him, she nodded. "I'd like the company, but I had planned to walk around the block tonight. I've been cooped up in the clinic all day and could use the fresh air."

"You mean *frigid* air?"

Laughing, her mood lightened. "You're right. I believe the temperature is going in the wrong direction for me. We're into March and not much change."

Morgan kept his gaze moving as they slipped between two buildings toward Rimrock Street. Gabe had talked to all his deputies about the threat to Griff, and possible danger to Carrie. They'd been taking turns keeping watch during her morning walk to the clinic, and evening walk home.

"Another month is what Enoch says." His eyes narrowed on movement toward the end of the street.

Her eyes twinkled at the mention of the older man. "Enoch seems to know how the weather works around here."

"I wouldn't argue with him. Did you hear we might be getting a veterinarian?"

"No. Did you hear that from Enoch, too?"

Morgan chuckled. "From Noah Brandt. He and Dax Pelletier have been trying to entice one to Splendor for a while now. They spoke with Bram MacLaren, who sent a telegram to his cousin in California. He graduated from a veterinary school in Scotland. Turns out he was a classmate who wants to come west."

Narrowing his gaze toward the end of the street once more, Morgan became certain someone waited near the corner of the last house on their right. The one belonging to Travis and Isabella. Shifting positions, he put Carrie on his left, away from the house.

"There's someone by the Dixons' house, Carrie. It may be best to cut back to your street."

"No. I want to walk to the end before returning home." She didn't say the reason for the detour would allow her to pass Griff's house. Maybe she'd get a brief glimpse of the man who'd captured her heart.

"If you're sure, stay a step behind me until we know who it is."

Several yards before the end of the street, a man stepped out, holding up his hand. "Evening, Morgan."

Carrie's stomach clenched at the sight of Isabella's husband. She wanted to give him a hard talk about responsibilities and commitment, knowing it wasn't her place.

"Travis. Haven't seen you in a while." Morgan held out a hand, stopping them. Carrie crossed her arms, glaring at him.

"I, uh...wanted to bring my pay to Isabella, but she's not home."

"She moved," Carrie blurted.

Taking a step closer, a brow lifted. "Moved? Where?"

"If you'd been here..." Her voice trailed off, knowing if he'd been home, Isabella wouldn't have had a reason to leave.

Morgan took pity on the man. He hoped Travis would come to his senses and accept the baby. "She's living with Gabe and Lena. They didn't want her to be alone, given her condition and all."

Stiffening at the obvious rebuke, Travis took a step toward Carrie, holding out something in his hand. "Would you give this to her? It's my pay."

"It would be better coming from you. She's been, well...she misses you."

Staring at his boots, he gave a slight shake of his head. "I'll speak with her at some point, but not tonight." Holding out the money once more, he let out a relieved breath when Carrie took it.

"It's not the money she wants, but I'll make sure she gets it."

Jaw clenched, he turned toward his horse standing several yards away.

"You aren't staying the night?" Carrie's strained words stopped him.

"No."

Swinging into the saddle, he kicked his horse, reining north toward the Pelletier ranch.

"Darn, stubborn man." Carrie stuffed the money into her reticule, her good mood vanishing.

"He'll come around."

"I don't know, Morgan. Isabella says he can be quite inflexible."

"Maybe he just needs…" The sharp crack of a gun sounded an instant before Morgan groaned, clutched his chest, and collapsed to the ground.

Chapter Fifteen

Carrie's scream echoed on the empty street. Dropping to her knees, shaky fingers checked the wound, relieved the bullet had gone through his back and out the front. Tugging up her dress, she tore a strip of cloth from her chemise, tearing it in half to press into the wound from both sides.

"Help! I need help!"

Someone dropped beside her as others gathered around.

"I'll carry him to the clinic, Carrie."

Startled, she whipped her head to find Griff, his body leaning into hers. "Griff..."

"I'll help." Morgan's good friend, Jonas, knelt down.

Before they could lift him, Clay McCord, carrying his bag, and Drake Ralston ran up. "Everyone get back except for Carrie and Drake." He motioned to his friend, who was already studying the wound.

"Gunshot, in and out, Clay. He's losing blood faster than he should with a shoulder wound. We have to get him to the clinic."

A wagon drew up beside them, Noah in the seat. "Get him in here."

Loading Morgan in the back, Clay and Drake jumped in with him, continuing to press against the two holes.

"I'll meet you there." Carrie rushed behind the wagon as Noah drove it up the street to the back of the clinic.

Glancing around for Griff, she couldn't see him. Her heart sank. He'd already left.

Refusing to allow herself a moment of remorse, she rushed to the back door, catching the key Clay tossed at her. "Please, everyone, give them plenty of space to carry Morgan inside."

The crowd complied, clearing a path so Morgan's closest friends, Tucker and Jonas, could carry him inside. Few noticed the tears spilling from the young men's eyes.

Closing the door behind them and the doctors, Carrie turned toward those who remained. "I'll get word out about his condition as soon as Doctor McCord gives his approval. What Morgan needs now is your prayers."

The lump in her throat threatened to choke her. They couldn't lose Morgan. He was too young, too vital, and too good a man to leave them now. That's when she felt the tears on her own cheeks.

Griff sat in the waiting room with Gabe, Tucker, and Jonas. The remaining deputies were searching the town for the shooter.

"They won't find him, Gabe. He's already out of town, hiding the same as all cowards."

"He believed Morgan was you, Griff."

"Yeah." Scrubbing a hand down his face, he thought of Carrie, and how close she'd come to being a victim. He had to get her out of town, to safety at the Pelletier ranch.

Getting her to agree wouldn't be easy. "He had to have hidden in one of Noah's empty houses. Is anyone checking inside?"

"Cole is searching each of the houses, as well as Travis's place." Gabe grimaced at the mention of Isabella's husband. The time had come for him to ride to Redemption's Edge and talk some sense into the man.

Shoving up, Griff stalked toward the door, stopping at Gabe's question.

"Where are you going?"

"To search, the same as your deputies."

Gabe stood, settling fisted hands on his hips. "There are enough people already."

"Until the shooter is found, you need as many people searching as possible." Reaching out to grasp the handle, he stepped back when the door flew open. Deputy Cole Santori entered, his features stoic.

"Cash found boot prints outside the back of the last empty house on the street, Gabe. There's mud inside, and one window was still open a crack. Enough to aim a six-shooter."

"Is Cash still there?"

"No. He, Beau, Zeke, and Hex are following the horse tracks out back of the house. They're pretty clear in the new snow."

Jonas stood, nothing of the tears remaining. "I'll join them, Gabe."

"No. You and Tucker need to stay here. When Morgan wakes up, he'll want to see friendly faces."

Nobody voiced their concern he might not survive. The door closing drew their attention. Griff had left.

"Stubborn cuss," Gabe hissed. "I'm going to find Dutch, Hawke, Caleb, Shane, and Mack. Cole, you're with me."

"Beth is also out there." Cole winced at the surprise on Gabe's face.

"How'd she know about the shooting?" His sister-in-law was staying at his house while his brother, Chan, escorted a prisoner to Deer Lodge. More than capable and an excellent shot, Gabe still had a hard time putting any woman in the face of danger.

Cole shrugged. "News travels fast, Sheriff. At night, you know how sound travels. She may have heard the shot."

Gabe thought his house too far away, but what did it matter. Beth was somewhere out there, determined, as always, to arrest the outlaw.

"Cole, I want you to find Beth and stick with her. Until Cash and the rest return, we can't be sure the shooter isn't still in town."

Groaning, he gave a terse nod before heading outside. Those in the room understood his reaction. Stubborn as any man, she held no concern for her own safety. A difficult trait for men who prided themselves on protecting women.

"I'll be back to check on Morgan." Buttoning his heavy coat, Gabe settled his hat low on his head.

Outside, the storm had picked up, the wind slapping him in the face. Dipping it down to protect his eyes, he plodded through the snow toward Noah's livery. The light still blazed from inside, flames from the forge serving to warm the large space his closest friend had owned for years.

Gabe missed the days he and Noah would take off to fish. They'd been close since running the streets of New York in knickers. The two had been inseparable, heading to college together before enlisting in the Northern cause. Afterward, they'd headed west. Noah stayed in Splendor, while Gabe continued his search, having no idea what he wanted. He'd ended up back with his friend, accepting the job as sheriff.

"Gabriel. Thought you'd be tracking the shooter."

"Wanted to thank you for bringing the wagon for Morgan."

Noah glanced up from his work, mouth quirking up at one corner. "Don't insult me."

Gabe understood. Noah never missed a chance to help those in the town both had grown to love.

"How's he doing?"

Leaning against a column, Gabe crossed his arms. "No word before I left the clinic. If Morgan dies..." Lifting his hat, he shredded fingers through his thick, dark hair.

Noah didn't need to ask to know his friend's meaning. "I'll help you."

"Cash found tracks inside and outside one of your vacant houses."

Noah straightened. Setting aside the tool he'd been shaping, the lines on his face tightened. "Which one?"

Gabe told him, shoving away from the column to look at the tool cooling on a bench. "He and a few other deputies are tracking him while the hoof prints are still visible in the snow."

Noah rubbed his jaw. "You gonna tell me the rest?"

Chuckling, Gabe took a quick look around, knowing no one else was in the building. "I can't shake the feeling there's more to this than we all believe."

Crossing his arms, Noah leaned a hip against the work table. "What bothers you?"

"Dirty Dave Dugan is who Griff believes is after him. Sheriff Sterling sent a telegram confirming the outlaw was in Big Pine, but rode out a week ago. He was heading west, toward Splendor. We've been scouring the town, showing the wanted poster, but no one's seen Dugan."

"Are you thinking he's not here, and someone else is after Griff?"

"I don't know what I'm thinking. Something's eating at my gut, and it's darn uncomfortable."

"Why does Griff believe Dugan's the shooter?"

Gabe explained about the death of Dugan's younger brother, how Griff had gunned the man down. "It's been several years, before he traveled to California, where he met the MacLarens."

"Outlaws aren't known for their patience. I'm surprised he waited this long."

Watching the growing storm, Gabe shoved both hands into his pockets. "I'm probably wrong. Guess I don't want to believe we can't locate a man we're sure is in Splendor."

"I'll come by the jail tomorrow to look at the wanted poster. Do you remember Dahlia? She works for Finn."

"She's the one who drew up the brands for you to look at."

"Right. Why don't you ask her to draw copies of the wanted poster? You could leave them around town so it's easier for someone to recognize him. Does he have a beard or mustache?"

"Both."

"Might have her draw a few without them. Easiest way for a man to change his look is to shave."

Gabe should've thought of this before now. "I'll talk to Finn. Thanks, Noah."

"I didn't do much."

"Except have the best idea I've heard since this started." Turning up his collar, Gabe walked into the gusting wind.

The snow stung his face, causing his eyes to water. Even stuffed inside his pockets, he could feel his hands go numb.

Reaching the telegraph office, he stepped onto the boardwalk, glad for the cover of its roof. Passing the Wild Rose, he pushed open the door of the jail, shivering as warmth surrounded him. Tossing wood into the stove, he considered making fresh coffee, deciding to wait until he'd finished his business.

The wanted poster was in his middle drawer, the first one in the stack. Holding it up, he tried to picture Dugan without the short beard and mustache. Folding it, he tucked it into an inside pocket.

Closing the door behind him, he decided to stop by the clinic before talking with Finn. The streets were empty, the storm keeping most everyone home. It reminded him of two Christmases past when the worst blizzard in recent memory held the town captive.

The quiet in the clinic hit Gabe square in the chest with thundering force. Neither Jonas nor Tucker looked up when he approached. A bad sign.

"Any word?"

Jonas's voice cracked on his reply. "Carrie came out a while ago. It doesn't look good."

"It isn't right, Gabe." Tucker swiped a hand across his mouth. "Morgan's the best of the three of us."

The pain in their voices punched him in the gut. In all his years in Splendor, he'd never lost a deputy. He didn't plan to lose one now.

Walking to the closed door of the examination room, he pulled the handle, opening it a couple inches. Clay and Drake bent over Morgan, working together to save the young deputy. Hearing the door open, Carrie looked up from her spot next to Clay, eyes showing the stress.

Gabe continued to watch until Doctor McCord raised his head. Gaze locking with Gabe's, he gave a slow shake of his head before resuming his work.

Heart sinking, Gabe found he couldn't move, as if him being there might help Morgan. Closing his eyes, he thought of Jonas and Tucker, how the loss of the third man in their circle would impact them.

A strong wave of exhaustion swept through him, clamping around his chest, tightening his throat, his breath growing labored. Stepping back, he drew the door toward him. Clay's voice stopped him.

"Get Reverend Paige, Gabe. And pray."

Chapter Sixteen

Griff swore in frustration. The group had circled the same area three times while Cash and Beau searched for more tracks, finding nothing. Not a surprise given the heavy snow.

"There's nothing we can do tonight." Cash swung into his saddle, reining the horse around. "We should head back to town before the storm gets any worse."

Griff couldn't argue with Cash's decision. They'd been out for close to three hours. Their horses were tired, as were the men. With the temperature dropping, they couldn't afford to stay out any longer. He moved his horse next to Cash.

"Do you think he circled back to town?"

Lifting a shoulder, Cash kept his attention focused on the trail before them. "Unless there's a cabin or cave out here, he'd have to go back. The way the storm is building, he'd freeze to death without protection."

The men settled into a tense silence. The killer was still out there somewhere, maybe with a gun trained on them. Griff doubted Dugan would come after him tonight, not with a posse ready to return fire.

Griff wondered if he was wrong about who was after him, then shook off his doubts. He'd known Dugan would track him down at some point, surprised the outlaw had waited so long. Before leaving California to make a new life in Montana with Bram and Thane MacLaren, Griff forced himself to stay on alert, expecting an attack from Dugan or any of half a dozen other outlaws.

"Carrie was there tonight." He spoke the words to no one in particular. "Dugan's known as a crack shot, always aiming to kill."

Cash glanced over at him. "You're saying if he wanted someone dead, they'd be dead?"

"That's what I'm saying. The man doesn't miss. Not when he has time to line up a shot."

"Might've realized the man wasn't you. He may have pulled his shot at the last second."

Griff already knew the bullet had been meant for him. He thought of Morgan and how he now fought for his life. It should've been him with Carrie, not the young deputy with an easy manner and quick intelligence.

"It's not your fault, Griff. All of it goes back to Dugan."

Griff swallowed the bile in his throat, understanding Cash's words but not accepting them. Guilt weighed heavy, sucking reason out of him.

"Whoever's stalking you, we *will* find him." The certainty in Cash's voice didn't surprise Griff. Confidence ran high in the men riding with him, as with all the men under Gabe's command.

Behind them, Hex and his brother, Zeke, spoke in low voices about the property they'd bought south of town. A thousand acres apiece.

Griff thought of the two hundred acres he'd purchased after the Boudreaux brothers closed on their property. Was it just a few days ago he'd signed the final documents? So much had happened in a short period of time, including his relationship with Carrie.

Darn if he didn't miss her more with each passing hour. The terror that had ripped through him finding her with a bleeding Morgan, confirmed the depth of his feelings. The knowledge angered him, but not for the reasons most would think. Their courting coincided with Dugan finding him, placing Carrie in danger.

Upon the posse's return to town, he'd speak with her, convince Carrie she'd be safer at the Pelletier ranch. It was a conversation Griff didn't look forward to.

Carrie sat alone in an empty examination room, tears streaming down her face. It wasn't often she felt such an acute sense of loss. Over the years, she'd convinced herself the death of each patient was God's will.

A soft knock had her swiping at the moisture on her face. Rising, she let out a ragged breath as she approached the door. Opening it, a whimpering sound escaped before she launched herself into Griff's arms.

They stood there for several moments before Carrie composed herself and stepped away. "Did you find him?"

"No. The snow covered the tracks before we could catch up to him." His thumb gently swiped away an errant tear. "Are you all right?"

"It's Morgan."

"From what Clay just told me, he's awake."

"What?" She shuffled around him, heading to the room where they'd been treating Morgan.

Inside, Jonas and Tucker stood by the bed, relief clear in their expressions. On the bed, face pale and etched with pain, Morgan tried to keep his eyes open. A few feet away, Clay and Drake rested against a counter, speaking in low voices. Walking around the bed, she joined them.

"How is he?"

Clay dragged a hand down his face, shaking his head. "Darndest thing. He wasn't responding at all. Drake and I were out of options. Then Morgan's eyes opened, and he asked why he was lying down."

"The bleeding stopped, some color is returning, and his pulse is strong. Guess it wasn't his time," Drake said. "Is there any coffee around here?"

"I'll make some." Taking another glance at Morgan, Carrie rushed out, almost running into Griff on her way to the stairs. "Come with me. The doctors want coffee."

With renewed energy, she hurried up the stairs to the small kitchen. Adding wood to the stove, she dumped the hours old coffee before starting a new pot.

Griff stood aside, watching her slender hands move quickly. They didn't speak as she finished, placing the pot on the stove.

"There should be enough for everyone." Reaching up, she opened the door to a cupboard, removing cups. "I can't believe Morgan is awake."

Griff moved closer, stroking a hand over her back. "It must've been hard. The waiting, I mean."

"He didn't respond, and the doctors couldn't stop the bleeding. I thought...we all thought...it was over."

"Appears God had other plans for Morgan."

She lifted her gaze to his, a tremulous smile brightening her face. He couldn't stop his head from lowering, his lips brushing across hers. The light touch seemed to reassure him.

"You need to pack clothes, Carrie. I'm taking you to the Pelletier ranch until we catch Dugan."

Moving away, her eyes grew wide. "It's not your decision."

"I've made it mine. Now that Morgan is doing better, I'll escort you home to get ready."

Crossing her arms, she lifted her chin. "The doctors need me here."

"I'll explain my reasons to Clay. He'll understand."

"Well, I don't."

Sighing, he reached out to touch her, but she stepped away. "You could've been injured or worse twice because of me. It would kill me if he succeeded." He glanced away for an instant before focusing back on the woman he'd come to love. "I need to know you're safe, Carrie."

Closing the distance between them, she reached up, stroking his cheek. "If you're staying in town, that's where I want to be."

"It's not safe."

"For you, either. More so, since you're his target." Raising on tiptoes, she placed a soft kiss on his mouth.

"All I'll do is worry if I'm at the ranch. Here, I'll have my work, a routine to keep my mind off Dugan."

As much as he hated her being a target, he understood. "We still can't be seen together."

"It didn't make any difference for Morgan. He was still mistaken for you."

Pacing away, he reeled around to face her. His voice rose with each word. "Dugan's bullet could've hit you instead of Morgan. Why can't you see this?"

"I do see it, Griff. I also understand Dugan wants you, not me. However, if it will make you feel better, I'll speak with Doctor McCord about leaving for a few days."

"Longer if needed. And *we* will speak with him together."

She set fisted hands on her hips. "No, Griff, we won't. I've been taking care of myself a long time. I don't need you to speak for me."

"My mistake," he muttered.

Carrie stepped toward him. "What was that?"

"You're strong and independent. There are times I forget how much."

Dropping her hands, she poured coffee into each of the cups, picking up two. "I'll give these to the doctors, then be back up."

Grabbing two more, Griff followed her downstairs. She handed two cups to Clay and Drake while Griff handed his to Jonas and Tucker, both watching Morgan drift back to sleep.

A rumbling sounded in Jonas's stomach, signaling how long it had been since he'd eaten. A moment later, Tucker's did the same.

"There's leftover stew in the kitchen. I can warm some up for each of you."

Jonas took another long swallow of coffee, lowering his cup. "Thank you, ma'am. That would be real good of you." Tucker nodded beside him.

"Stay put and I'll bring it down to you." When Carrie headed upstairs, Griff stepped closer to Clay.

"I want Carrie to stay at the Pelletier ranch for a while. After tonight, I need to know she's safe. She's worried about her job here."

"Georgina will be back from Big Pine tomorrow. We can get by without Carrie for a few days. Even if it's longer, we aren't going to hire anyone else." Clay took a sip from his cup, grinning. "She sure makes better coffee than any of us."

Carrie appeared a few minutes later with a bowl in each hand. "Here you are." She pulled two biscuits from her pocket. "There's jam on those."

A broad grin spread across Tucker's face. "Thank you, ma'am."

Clay set down his empty cup. "Why don't you boys sit down in the waiting room to eat? Doctor Ralston or I will let you know when he wakes up again."

Carrie waited until the young men left the room before approaching Clay. "May I speak with you a moment, Doctor?"

He turned to face her. "What is it?"

"Would you mind if I took a few days off to stay with Rachel?"

Clay sent a look at Griff, not letting on they'd already spoken. "I think it's a real fine idea. We don't want to treat one of our nurses for a gunshot wound."

Clearing her voice, she shot a look between the men, neither meeting her gaze. "Well, then. I guess it's settled. Would tomorrow be too soon?"

"Tomorrow is fine. Doctor Ralston is here, and Georgina will return to town tomorrow on the stage from Big Pine."

"If you don't mind, I'll get my coat and go home."

Clay nodded. "Be careful, Carrie. You're important to this clinic, and a good friend."

Escorting her outside, Griff slipped her arm through his. Keeping her close, neither spoke as they passed the two houses between the clinic and Carrie's.

"Do you want to come in for a bit?"

"Yes, but I'd better not. Too many eyes watching." Turning her toward him, he bent to press his mouth to hers. One kiss turned to two, then three before he straightened. "I'll be here early to take you to the ranch."

"I'll be ready." Watching him leave, Carrie couldn't stop herself from wondering where the relationship with Griff was headed. How serious was he? How serious was she?

Closing the door, she leaned against it. There'd be no answers until the threat to Griff ended.

Chapter Seventeen

Gabe stood at the bar, waiting for Finn to finish a discussion with his bartender. In his pocket was the folded wanted poster for Dirty Dave Dugan. At mid-morning, he didn't expect to see Dahlia, or any of the girls who worked upstairs.

He hadn't been inside Finn's for weeks, didn't even know if Dahlia still worked here. The more Gabe considered Noah's idea, the more it made sense. He hadn't considered Dugan would change his appearance by shaving off his lush mustache.

"What can I get you to drink, Sheriff?"

"Nothing for me, Finn. Does Dahlia still work for you?"

Giving Gabe a considering look, he raised a brow. "You want a room upstairs?"

He almost laughed at the ridiculous idea. "Just want to speak with her. I'd appreciate it if you'd ask her to come down."

"Dahlia isn't too, uh...welcoming in the morning. Can this wait until after lunch?"

"Afraid not. This has to do with the man who shot Deputy Wheeler last night."

Finn's mouth twisted in disgust. "Heard he bushwhacked Morgan and Miss Galloway. A man like him deserves no mercy. I'll get Dahlia."

Tugging the poster from his pocket, he set it on the bar. Gabe shifted to look out the window. The storm had passed to reveal a sun as bright as you'd ever see in western Montana. The rays beat down on the ground, melting the snow to create foot deep ruts. The mud was high enough to seep into the boots of those foolish enough to cross the street. Not even outlaws came out on days such as this.

"She'll be right down. Might as well have a seat." Finn motioned to a nearby table, motioning to his bartender for two coffees.

Gabe grabbed the poster from the bar, wrapping his fingers around it. Finn and Dahlia would hear what he wanted at the same time. Taking the cup from the bartender's hand, he took a sip, wincing at the bitterness. He'd become used to the coffee he had shipped from his hotels in New York. Finn's coffee couldn't compare.

Gabe heard Dahlia's heavy footfalls on the stairs, and a loud yawn she couldn't stifle. Part of her hair was held together in a messy bun, the rest loose around her shoulders. It struck Gabe how her appearance, although disheveled, didn't show the rigid, deep lines common to women who'd practiced her profession for several years. He knew she'd been working a good, long time. Standing, he pulled out a chair.

"Thank you, Sheriff." She looked at the bartender. "Can I get a whiskey?" Straightening her skirt, she placed one arm on the table, resting her chin in the palm of her hand. "Finn says you wanted to talk to me."

Unfolding the poster, he slid it to her. "We're looking for this man."

Studying it, she lifted her head. "I heard. He the one who shot the deputy last night?"

"We believe so. It's likely Dugan has been in town for a while. There's a chance he's shaved off his mustache and beard, and cut his hair. I know you can draw, Dahlia." He let his meaning sink in.

"You want me to draw him without the hair on his face?" She took the whiskey from the bartender's hand, tossing it back and swallowing.

"Can you do it?"

"It'll take a day. Come back this afternoon and I'll have it for you."

Leaving the remaining coffee in the cup, Gabe shoved his chair back and stood. "I'll see you in a few hours. Thank you, Dahlia. Finn, I appreciate your help."

"Carrie's welcome to stay as long as needed, Griff. We always have room." Dax stood beside him, both watching Rachel and Ginny Pelletier speaking with her.

"She wanted to stay in town."

"Rachel would've said the same if I'd become a target. What do you know about Dugan?"

Griff explained his history with the outlaw, Sheriff Sterling's telegram, and how Gabe and his deputies had been canvassing the town.

"So far, nothing. Last night, he shot one of the deputies."

Dax's brows rose. "Who?"

"Morgan Wheeler. He almost didn't make it. Now it's a matter of avoiding infection."

"You said Carrie was with him when the attack occurred?"

"Gabe asked all the deputies to watch over her. Morgan saw her walking alone after leaving the clinic. He offered to escort her home."

"Dugan thought Morgan was you."

"That's what we all believe. Cash found tracks inside and outside one of Noah's houses. Several of us followed, but lost the trail when the storm worsened. I have a hard time believing no one in town has seen him." He clasped Dax on his back. "Thank you for helping us out."

"Anytime, Griff."

Approaching Carrie, he held out a hand. "I'm leaving. Come outside with me?"

Threading her fingers through his, they stepped onto the porch. The clear sky showed no signs of an approaching storm.

"You'll be careful riding back to town?"

Sliding a finger down her cheek, Griff cupped her chin. "Yes."

His voice had grown husky with need. Gaze wandering over her face, he had a hard time believing a woman as wonderful as Carrie would chose a future with him. She was goodness and light to the darkness he'd carried with him for years. The woman he'd searched for through all the miles he'd traveled, the people he'd hunted down or killed. All justified. All taking a little more from his soul.

Bending down, he covered her mouth with his. This time, he lingered, the kisses becoming more heated as his hands ran over her back. He felt her shiver, although he didn't believe it was from the cold.

Although not ready to let her go, he knew it would be safer to travel in daylight. Lifting his mouth from hers, he rested his forehead against hers, their heated breaths mingling.

"I should go."

Her fingers dug into the thick fabric covering his arms. "When will you return?"

"When the threat is gone."

Carrie expected the vague answer, even if it wasn't what she wanted to hear. "Be safe, Griffin MacKenzie. I'm not finished with you yet."

Judge Hoodoo praised his luck at the bright sun and clear skies. Whistling, he used a light hand to guide his horse out of Moosejaw toward Big Pine. His horse struggled through the deep snow, picking its way around frozen brush and rocks the size of a large bull. He couldn't find it within himself to care.

Leaving Moosejaw several miles behind, Hoodoo stayed watchful for both Dugan and three bank robbers, who might or might not be women. The one sitting in jail refused to talk. Not a word since her arrest. The judge had no doubt her compadres would attempt to break her out before or during the trial. If he didn't have some place to be, Hoodoo would've stayed to watch the fireworks.

Hoodoo thought of the days ahead, knowing they could be his last. Fearing death had ceased the day his wife died. He'd willingly accept his own demise if it meant the man who ended her life went to hell with him. Until then, he'd enjoy each day.

He'd heard of Sheriff Parker Sterling. With over thirty years upholding the law, the man had a solid reputation covering several states. Incorruptible, Hoodoo believed the man should be featured in dime novels instead of those with less character.

A flash of metal to the right caught his attention. Drawing his gun, he slipped to the ground, using his horse as cover. Watching over the saddle, he saw the flash again.

He was grateful his pale dun gelding didn't stand out in the snow. Continuing to walk alongside his horse, he pulled back on the reins, slowing their pace. Seeing a flash again, he stopped, deciding it best to let whoever was out there ride on.

After several minutes without seeing further flashes, Hoodoo mounted, settling his body into the saddle. From what he could figure, there were still several miles to Big Pine.

Staring into the distance, he groaned. A dark wave of storm clouds moved in from the southwest. It wouldn't be long before the massive thunderstorm blocked the sun, and the warm day would end.

With a sense of urgency, he urged his gelding into a trot. Looking north, he no longer saw the flashes of light. Maybe he'd been imagining another rider.

He had several more miles to cover before reaching Big Pine, and not much time until the storm opened up. Hoodoo's initial joy disappeared, and he no longer whistled.

Griff spent the remainder of his day working in the office, completing two contracts, and finalizing details on the changes Isabella requested. Folding the papers, he slid them into his pocket briefcase.

He'd volunteered to meet her at Gabe's house, figuring if anyone saw her entering the law offices they might form incorrect conclusions. Isabella and Travis didn't need gossip implying they were planning to end their marriage. Travis may not have returned for more than to deliver his earnings to Isabella, but neither spoke of divorce.

When delivering Carrie to the Pelletier ranch, Griff had asked to speak with Travis. The man had refused. He wouldn't be sharing this with Isabella.

Stepping onto the boardwalk, he looked up, his gaze locking on the building clouds. Dark and ominous, they promised another fierce storm.

Collecting his horse, Griff didn't rush on his way to the Evans' home. The house, reminiscent of the stately manors in exclusive neighborhoods of New York, was tucked into a thick stand of trees not far from town. Smaller than its eastern cousins, Griff knew it had six bedrooms and three water closets.

Reining up at the front of the house, he dismounted, taking his time. The door opened before he reached the covered porch, Isabella facing him.

"Hello, Griff. Thank you for coming." The dark shadows under her eyes, sallow expression, and splotchy complexion indicated how the separation from Travis affected her. Griff wondered if Travis experienced any regrets.

"It's always a pleasure visiting Gabe and Lena's home. You look wonderful, as always."

"Oh, Griff. You have a way with words. Even when they're false, they raise a woman's spirits."

Following her into the parlor, he waved off her offer of a drink. "How do you feel?"

"As you might expect. The doctor says I'm fine. Here," she touched her chest, "not quite as good." Sitting, she straightened her dress before meeting his gaze. "Do you have the updated documents?"

Taking the pocket briefcase from his coat, Griff removed the papers, unfolding them. "Please read these over carefully. I want to confirm the contents are what you intended."

Her hand shook as she took the documents from him. Standing, he made a slow turn around the room, giving her time.

Griff studied several portraits he assumed were from the Evans home in New York. The shelves were filled with books on botany, geography, and historic figures. A two-volume set on the American Revolution caught his attention. He made a mental note to ask Gabe about borrowing them.

"I believe this covers everything, Griff." Standing, she walked to the desk, withdrawing a pen. Signing and dating the document, she sat down. "There is one more item I'd prefer you handle."

Taking the documents from her outstretched hand, he set them aside. "Whatever you need, Isabella."

Taking a deep breath, she exhaled slowly. Several minutes passed as she considered what to say. Coming to a decision, she squared her shoulders, her eyes glistening with emotion.

"I'd like you to draw up papers."

"For what?"

"My divorce."

Chapter Eighteen

Redemption's Edge Ranch

Carrie buttoned her coat, added a wool hat, and headed outside. She'd helped Rachel with breakfast and cleaned the kitchen, all while glancing outside to the bright sun and clear sky. It had been hard to watch Griff ride away, leaving her safe while he headed into danger.

Standing on the porch, she breathed in the cold air in an attempt to clear her head. She continued to think about Morgan's shooting, the look on his face as she worked to stop the bleeding. A look telling her he thought the end was near. Without the quick actions of Clay and Drake, he might've been.

Carrie didn't look forward to tonight and the expected nightmare. The image of the first bullet whizzing between her and Griff while they stood on her porch haunted her day and night. She didn't doubt last night's shooting would be the subject of more nightmares.

Releasing a resigned breath, she took the steps to the ground, heading to a corral where three men worked with an untamed horse. She recognized them as Billy Zales, Bram MacLaren, and Travis. Her stomach lurched at the pain he'd caused Isabella.

Avoiding a series of ruts filled with melted snow, she stopped at the fence, captivated at the way the three worked together. Bram held one rope, Billy another, as Travis secured the saddle around the mare's girth.

"You ready?" Billy asked Travis. Carrie assumed Isabella's husband would be the one to tame the animal.

Taking the reins from Billy's hand, Travis gripped a handful of the mare's mane. His movements were smooth, confident, as he swung into the saddle. A long moment passed before he gave a clipped nod, resulting in Bram and Billy releasing the ropes.

A tense silence blanketed the corral as neither horse nor man moved. Carrie gripped the top rail, wanting to step onto the lowest rung, waiting to see what happened next. She didn't wait long.

An explosion of raw power almost dislodged Travis from the saddle. The mare bucked several times, back legs kicking, before swinging her body left, then right.

It did no good. Travis held on, both hands gripping the saddlehorn.

Carrie's hands gripped the top rail, heart pounding against her ribs, breath hitching. She'd never watched a wild horse being tamed. She couldn't look away.

The mare stilled, making Carrie believe the fight was over. Travis made no move to dismount. Animal and man waited. Seconds passed before the mare exploded into the air again, startling Carrie. Bram and Billy didn't react from where they stood outside the corral several feet from her.

The mare reacted to the weight on her back the same as when Travis first mounted. Bucking, kicking, swinging one way, then the other. Nothing worked to dislodge the cowboy whose attention didn't waver from the task.

His fierce expression reminded Carrie of a painting hanging in an office back east. The figure, a cowboy with deep lines etched into his face, steely gaze, and coil of rope on one shoulder, stared at the artist. He was a hard man, living in a world defined by work few men back east would understand. At the time, she wondered why any man would choose such a life. Now she understood. Such men weren't meant to wear a suit or work behind a desk.

As the thought took hold, Carrie realized Griff could fit in either world. The Range Detective tracking down and arresting outlaws, and the sharp-witted attorney. A gunslinging lawyer. Her mouth twisted into a wry grin.

No matter how the mare responded, she couldn't dislodge Travis. The man had made up his mind the horse wouldn't triumph. He'd be the victor. Carrie wondered if he approached Isabella's condition in the same way. If so, it wouldn't end well for either of them.

"What do you think, Carrie?" Rachel stopped next to her.

"Incredible. A wild horse and determined man battling each other."

Rachel considered Carrie's words, agreeing with her. "Most times, the horse bucks off whoever's on their back."

"Travis appeared in total control."

Rachel's gaze tracked Travis as he guided the mare around the corral. "He's one of the best, as are Bram and Billy."

Carrie faced her friend. "Has Travis talked at all about Isabella?"

Rachel's features sobered. "He's not one to talk about anything personal. I know Dax has spoken with him. Dax isn't pleased with Travis walking out on his wife. Neither am I."

"Do you think he'll go back?"

"No idea, but I know he misses Isabella."

"How so?"

"He sits alone to eat his meals. After supper, he walks around the barn and corrals until exhaustion forces him to bed. Dax says he rarely talks to anyone, not even Billy and Bram. He and Billy have been close for a long time, but more like father and son. I doubt Travis confides in him."

"Or anyone."

Rachel nodded. "True. How is Isabella doing?"

"She's living with Lena and Gabe."

"I heard."

"The warm smile is gone. Their separation has taken its toll on her." Carrie glanced into the corral, where Travis slid to the ground and walked toward Bram and Billy. "My heart breaks for both of them."

"Dax and Luke have talked about bringing Isabella out here, forcing them to talk. I'm not certain that's such a good idea."

"I don't know. A short visit of a few days might be the push Travis needs."

"As long as Dax and Luke don't force a conversation." Rachel's lips pressed together.

"Agreed."

Rachel leaned against the fence, her body relaxed. "Now tell me about you and Griff."

"Me and Griff?"

"I've known you a long time, Carrie. You've never looked at a man the way you do Griff. Not even Shane Banderas."

Carrie motioned for Rachel to follow her. When a good distance away from the men, she looked at her friend. "I was never in love with Shane."

"And you are in love with Griff?"

A smile formed on Carrie's face. "Yes, I am."

They walked several yards before Rachel asked the question niggling at her. "Have you told him?"

"Absolutely not. What if he doesn't feel the same?" She shivered at the thought. "It would be too humiliating."

"Oh, Carrie. I doubt you'd be humiliated. Not from the way he acts when around you."

Thinking of her time with Griff, she couldn't argue with Rachel. He was always attentive, treated her with respect, and made her feel treasured. Shane had been the same, except he'd always been distant, as if he wasn't truly with her. She'd learned it was because he wasn't. His thoughts had been consumed with his first love, Angela Baldwin.

"You may be right. I'm still not going to tell him how I feel. As I recall, you didn't say anything to Dax until he admitted his feelings."

"True. I do hope when he comes to take you back to town, he'll have time to stay longer than a few minutes."

Carrie stopped, her gaze narrowing on Rachel. "You aren't to question him."

"I won't question him about the two of you, but I am interested in learning more about him. After all, one of my best friends is in love with him."

Carrie kept thinking about Rachel's words as she helped bring in the laundry. The building storm clouds brought an urgency to the chore. Shining Star, Billy's wife, worked beside her, their young son in a basket at her feet. They didn't speak, both concentrating on their work.

It didn't stop Carrie from considering her feelings for Griff. She cared deeply about him, enjoyed their time together, and always looked forward to seeing him again. Did it mean she was in love with him?

The sound of a rider approaching caught her attention. Walking to the corner of the house, her heart flipped. Griff reined up by the corral. She couldn't stop her feet from moving. Had it only been hours since he'd brought her to the ranch?

"Hello, Griff."

Turning at her voice, a broad smile brightened his face. "There you are."

"What brings you back so soon?"

Taking Carrie's arm, he guided her toward the porch. Confirming they were alone, he lowered his voice.

"I met with Isabella today. She made some additional decisions and asked me to discuss them with Travis."

"Will what you have to tell him help their situation?"

"No, sweetheart, it won't." Griff glanced behind her, making a sweep of the area. "Do you know where he is?"

"I believe he's in the barn. I'll go with you."

He gripped her arm again. "I'm afraid you can't. What I have to say is for him only."

Biting her lower lip, she gave a slow nod of understanding. "Did she give him an ultimatum?"

"Her instructions are confidential. I will say her decision was a surprise to me." The resignation in Griff's voice worried her.

"Well, I'll leave you to find him. Will you have time to say goodbye before you leave?"

Taking her hand in his, he squeezed. "Yes."

Carrie watched as he crossed the distance to the barn, and entered.

It took a moment before Griff's eyes adjusted to the shadowy interior. Off in a corner sat Travis, his head bent as he worked on a piece of rope. He glanced up when Griff approached. Tossing the rope aside, he stood, shaking the hand extended toward him.

"Is there a reason for this visit?"

Griff reached into a pocket, removing an envelope. "Isabella asked me to bring this to you."

Travis stared at it, making no move to take it from Griff.

"She wrote a letter to you. It's important you read it."

Sighing, Travis took the envelope. His eyes lit on his wife's handwriting, a sharp pain cutting through him. Turning away, he tore the paper, removing the letter.

It wasn't at all what he expected.

Dearest Travis,

First, I must apologize for allowing myself to be with child, although it wasn't my intention to do so. Your anger and resentment were expected. What had been a surprise was your abandonment. It's been three weeks with no word, and I must conclude you have no intention of returning home.

You must know how much I love you. Still, it appears my love isn't enough to keep you with me. Because of this, I've made a difficult and painful decision.

I've asked Griff MacKenzie to prepare papers to dissolve our marriage.

Travis stopped, whirled around to face Griff, but said nothing. The pain in his chest hurt so much, he found it hard to breathe. Heart pounding, he continued reading the letter.

I doubt this will come as a surprise to you. Please understand my love for you is true and will never waver.

There will never be another man for me, yet I believe the time has come to set you free. Given your decision to never have children, I don't see how you could ever be happy with me once the baby comes. I will be moving to another house, as the one we've shared has too many wonderful memories.

Please stay safe. Someday, I pray you'll think of me with love.

Yours always,
Isabella

A curse Griff had never heard Travis utter echoed in the cavernous space. Crumbling the paper in his hand, he threw it down before stalking to a stall.

Leading his sorrel gelding, Banjo, outside, Travis didn't take the time to tack him up before swinging onto the animal's back. With a cry ripping from his throat, he urged Banjo into a run, reining him straight toward Splendor.

Chapter Nineteen

Hearing Travis's shout, Carrie came running toward Griff, Rachel close behind. Placing a hand on his arm, she tore her gaze from the retreating horse to Griff.

"What was that about? Is Isabella all right?" Lines of worry etched her face, more prominent around her mouth and eyes.

"Travis didn't say, but I believe he's heading into town to speak with Isabella."

Carrie's mouth twisted, her brows lifting. "And you have no idea why?"

Rachel stood beside her, showing the same suspicion.

"Isabella wanted to meet with me earlier today. She'd made some decisions that impact Travis. After explaining her instructions, he left without a word of explanation. It's nothing I can share with anyone else."

"Isabella and the baby are all right?"

Threading his fingers through hers, he squeezed. "They're fine. It appears they'll be talking for the first time in three weeks. My guess is a resolution to their differences isn't far away."

Rachel looked between them, landing on Griff. "Anything more on the person who shot Morgan?"

"Nothing I'm aware of. Gabe still has his deputies searching in and around town. He seems to hide out during the day, saving his malice for night. He's also asked a woman to redraw Dugan's wanted poster image without the mustache and beard."

Rachel offered a knowing nod. "Probably Dahlia at Finn's. She's helped the sheriff before when Zeke was attacked."

"Did her drawing help?" Carrie asked.

"Sure did. They caught the person responsible, in part because of Dahlia's help. I need to get back in the house. Are you staying for supper, Griff? There'll be plenty."

He felt Carrie's hand tighten on his arm. Removing his hat, he ran fingers through his dark, wavy hair, meeting her expectant gaze. He swept the area for any sign he may have been followed from town. Putting those on the ranch in danger was what he'd been trying to avoid.

As if reading his thoughts, Carrie cupped his cheek with her free hand. "I doubt the shooter will come after you on the ranch. Too many people will be watching for him."

"She's right, Griff. You're probably safer here than anywhere else."

He didn't hesitate long. "Thank you, Rachel. Supper sounds good."

The food was excellent, as always. Griff didn't hesitate when Rachel offered seconds. When he thought he couldn't eat another bite, she set a dried apricot pie and canned cherry pie on the table.

Both pans were empty twenty minutes later, along with two pots of coffee. Waiting until the table was cleaned and dishes finished, Griff took Carrie's arm, guiding her to the porch.

The temperature had dropped at least ten degrees since they'd gone inside for supper. They sat next to each other on the wood swing.

"Why won't you accept Dax's offer of staying the night, Griff?"

He knew she'd ask. There wasn't a good answer. Not one she'd understand.

"The last two attacks have been between eight and nine at night. I want to be in town during that time."

"Gabe knows this, right?"

"He does."

"Why do you need to be there?" The words left her mouth when the answer became clear. "Because you're the target," she whispered.

Taking her hand in his, Griff gave a slight squeeze. "This has gone on too long, Carrie. I want it to end."

"Have you considered it might end in your death?"

He stayed silent for a long time, his gaze locked on something far in the distance. "It might."

Not responding, she followed his gaze, seeing nothing. Her throat felt rough, as if she'd been caught in a dust storm with her mouth open. His answer provided no comfort. Griff seemed not to care about his own safety, how his death would impact those who cared for him. How it would affect her.

Carefully tugging her hand from his, she stood, walking to the porch rail, resting her hands on the top. No words passed between them as she came to terms with his intention to act as bait to draw Dugan out. This side of Griff was new to Carrie. She didn't know what to think of it.

Having been born and reared in New York, she wasn't accustomed to the type of men who faced danger straight on. Some did what they believed was right, regardless of the possible threat to them. Griff was one of those men. Coming up behind her, Carrie felt his hands rest on her waist.

"What are you thinking?"

"I don't want you making yourself a target. It's Gabe's job to find and arrest Dugan, not yours."

"I'm the best chance Gabe has of drawing Dugan out. He's watching and waiting for me. It's time to end this."

Turning to face Griff, she gripped his upper arms. "If you're not there, Dugan will get tired of waiting and ride out. You'd be safe."

"You're wrong. Dugan won't leave town until he's arrested or one of us is dead. This is the best way."

"Not if you die trying to catch him. I don't understand why it has to be you, Griff."

Leaning back, he stared into eyes filled with worry. He hated causing her such pain. Living in the frontier meant dealing with men such as Dugan, especially someone with Griff's background. Could he continue to cause her such agony? Dropping his hands, he took a step away.

He hadn't intended for this discussion to happen today. Griff had hoped to never have it, but Carrie was consumed by worry. Griff didn't want her to live her life anxious about whether he'd come home or not. Some women were strong enough to deal with threats to their husband's life. Some weren't. Carrie appeared to be the latter.

She'd be better off with a shopkeeper or doctor, instead of a lawyer who carried a gun because of his past. If there were children, the fear she showed tonight would never end. Eventually, she'd leave, unable to come to terms with potential threats to his life.

Perhaps it was for the best to let her go now, when they could walk away without causing too much hurt.

"Sit down, Carrie." He motioned to the swing. With a lifting of her brow, she did as he ordered.

Dread filled her. The look in his eyes, determination mixed with regret, scared her. Forcing her gaze to meet his, her heart beat wildly in her chest. She knew what he would say before he opened his mouth. When she patted the seat beside her, he shook his head, confirming his intentions.

"I've been considering this for a while Carrie. Ever since the first shot at your house." Swallowing, he searched for the right words. "Dugan will not be the last man to come after me. He's one of many who want me dead. I know you see me as a small town lawyer, but my life has been more complicated than that."

Knowing what had to be said, he forced out the words. "It would be best to not see each other any longer. My life, well...it doesn't suit a woman such as you." The flash of pain on her face couldn't be missed, but it was too late to take the words back.

Carrie stared at him for several long minutes, letting the meaning of his statement take hold. Attempting to respond, she found her throat tight, jaw locked in place. Forcing herself to stand, she lifted her chin in an action of defiance.

"It seems you've made the decision for both of us. Our courtship is over without discussion." Her voice didn't falter, for which she was grateful. "Thank you for allowing me to be a part of your life, even if the time was incredibly short. Goodbye, Griffin MacKenzie." Whirling around, she took measured steps to the door, gripping the latch.

"Carrie, wait."

She didn't turn around or glance over her shoulder. Doing so, looking into his eyes, would've broken the last thread of her composure. Carrie refused to allow Griff to see how his ending their courtship affected her. Pain, sharp as a doctor's scalpel, sliced through her. Each step became more difficult than the last. Each breath scorched her already damaged heart.

Drawing the door closed behind her, she headed down the hall to her bedroom, anger increasing with each step. She loved him, and knew Griff loved her. Carrie didn't have to ask to know he was doing this to spare her pain in the future. Throwing the door open, she stomped into her bedroom.

"Stupid, stupid, stupid man." Tossing her coat on a chair, she paced the small bedroom, refusing to let a single tear fall. Sitting on the edge of the bed, she covered her face, letting the mix of emotions burst forth in a frustrated growl. She hoped no one else heard, although the relief she felt was worth it.

Carrie refused to believe Griff no longer wanted her. Given his past professions, he'd made up his mind she couldn't handle men such as Dugan hunting him.

"He's wrong. So very wrong about me." Jumping up, she went to the window, looking toward the barn in time to see Griff lead his roan gelding, Thunder, outside.

Stomach clenching, she wrapped both arms around her waist. For an instant, she wondered if he no longer desired her. Then she saw him look toward her bedroom, faltering when seeing her at the window. Lifting his hand, he waved a goodbye, one she couldn't return.

Dropping his hand, Griff swung into the saddle, took one last look at her, then left for town.

The impact of what he'd done hit Griff less than a mile from the ranch. A sorrow he'd never experienced wrapped around him, stealing his breath and crushing his heart.

Falling in love with Carrie had been easy. Smart, funny, sweet, and beautiful. What man wouldn't want to call her his? He'd wanted her from the start. Still wanted her.

Someone as wonderful as her deserved a better future, with a man not tainted by past actions.

He refused to offer her a life guarding their family against ghosts from his past. How could he live with himself if anything happened to her?

Griff recalled the day she and four other women had arrived from New York. His gaze had latched onto her, and to this day, he hadn't tired of the view. He'd been half in love with Carrie before ever inviting her to supper.

When she'd made known her interest in Shane, Griff had accepted any opportunity with her had been lost. Not long after, the woman Shane had loved most of his life arrived in Splendor, and everything changed. Griff had been given a second chance, never intending to walk away.

So why had he ended their courtship? Telling himself not being together would keep Carrie safe—now and in the future—seemed weak as he thought back on the decision. The intense hurt on her face had nearly gutted him.

She'd put up a brave stance, doing her best not to let his betrayal show. Griff hadn't been with anyone else, yet it was a betrayal just as deep. The disloyalty came from admitting his deep feelings for Carrie, his desire to seek a future with her. It hadn't been a marriage proposal, yet he'd taken the declaration seriously, as had Carrie. Tonight, he'd snatched it away and left, leaving his heart behind.

"You're a fool, MacKenzie." He reined up.

Sitting atop his horse, he lifted his head to an almost cloudless night, wrestling with what to do. Griff knew he should turn around and ride back. But he wouldn't. He'd made his decision, and he'd live with it. At least until Dugan had been captured or killed.

<h1 align="center">Chapter Twenty</h1>

"Dahlia did a real good job, Griff." Gabe slid the image of Dave Dugan, without his mustache and beard, across the desk.

Studying the image, Griff had hoped for a hint of recognition. Maybe a man he'd seen in one of the restaurants or saloons, walking on the boardwalk, or in the St. James. Frustrated, he handed it back to Gabe. "With or without the facial hair, I haven't seen him in Splendor. When Dugan and I squared off a few years ago, he had the mustache and beard. Have you shown it to the bartenders?"

"Not yet. Dahlia brought it over a little before you walked into the jail. I intend to start on the Wild Rose tonight, then head to the Dixie and Finn's."

"What about Ruby's Palace?"

"I'll show it to Ruby. She's always downstairs, and watches every customer. The woman doesn't forget a face."

Griff had heard the same. "Do you mind if I go with you?"

"Not at all." Gabe folded the drawing and checked his six-shooter, a habit since the war. Sliding it back into its holster, he grabbed his coat and hat. "Let's get going."

The boardwalk was empty, not unusual in temperatures below ten degrees. In contrast, the Wild

Rose didn't have a single empty table, and there were no spaces at the bar.

Gabe showed the drawing around. In contrast to the original wanted poster, several studied it. A few thought they'd seen Dugan, but couldn't remember where.

Gabe and Griff got the same response at the Dixie and Finn's. As at the Wild Rose, several men vowed to watch for the outlaw.

"The drawing was a good idea, Gabe. Did you notice the last man we showed it to in Finn's? He recognized Dugan. I'm certain of it." They walked together toward Ruby's Palace.

"Agreed. Have you seen the man before?"

Griff shook his head. "But I rarely go into Finn's."

Gabe raised a hand when he spotted Caleb Covington walking toward them. He'd been a Texas Ranger before coming to Splendor to take a job as a deputy.

"Gabe. You're out late tonight." Caleb nodded at Griff.

"I've been showing the new drawing of Dugan to people at the saloons. There's something I need you to do. The last man we showed it to at Finn's didn't say anything, but I'm certain he recognized Dugan. He's sitting at the table to the left as you enter. Right by the window. Bright red hair with streaks of white, beard, and handlebar mustache."

"You want me to watch him?" Caleb asked.

"Try to sit at his table. Find out what you can about him."

An interested gleam showed in Caleb's eyes. "I'll head right over there, Sheriff."

"Let me know what you learn."

Watching Caleb cross the street to Finn's, Gabe and Griff continued on to Ruby's. They hadn't gotten fifty yards before Caleb called after them.

"Was he gone?" Gabe asked.

Breathing heavily, he shook his head. "I didn't need to sit at his table. One look and I recognized him."

Gabe shot a look at Griff before his attention shifted back to Caleb. "Who is he?"

"Have you heard of Judge Hoodoo Hardin?"

Rubbing a brow, Gabe's eyes widened. "The judge from Denver?"

"Right. He's originally from Texas. That's how I learned about him. As hard a man on criminals as you'll ever meet. He'd just as soon hang them as send them to prison. The judge is also a dead shot with a six-shooter or rifle. I heard he's been a judge in Denver the last few years."

Griff looked behind Caleb toward Frontier Street and Finn's. "What's he doing here?"

Scratching the back of his neck, Caleb gave a slow shake of his head. "I wouldn't know. It seems odd, though."

Gabe's attention was drawn upwards in time to see a shooting star. Perhaps it was a sign they were getting somewhere. He hoped so. "I know the sheriff in Denver. I'll send him a telegram to see if he knows anything."

"Now that you know who he is, I'll go back to Finn's. I'd like to know if he's passing through or planning to stay for a while."

"Thanks, Caleb. Let me know what you learn. Tomorrow morning is soon enough."

"Will do, Gabe."

The sheriff looked at Griff. "Have you heard of Judge Hoodoo Hardin?"

"He's a legend in Texas and Colorado. If you're guilty, you do not want him as the judge. If you're innocent, you still don't want him. The man has one verdict. Guilty. He figures if you've been arrested, you're probably guilty."

Gabe started toward Ruby's. "And the people still want him?"

"No one wants him. It's oftentimes out of their hands. I don't know how he got the job in Denver. Connections is my guess." Griff's thoughts began to wander to Carrie. He quickly pulled them back to focus on Dugan, and now, Judge Hardin. That's when he spotted him.

Reacting on impulse, he shoved Gabe aside while pulling the gun from its holster. "Get down."

They hit the ground at the same time two bullets slammed into the building next to them. "It's Dugan. He's across the street in the doorway of the meat market."

Another bullet hit within inches of Griff's head. "Cover me, Gabe. I'm going to circle around behind him. Ready?"

"Go!" Gabe rose, aiming for the meat market, and fired until he needed to reload his revolver. Sliding bullets into the cylinder, he began shooting again.

"Don't shoot, Gabe."

Lowering his six-shooter, he didn't stand until Griff came out the front door of the meat market. Gabe met him in the middle of the street.

"Did you see him?"

Griff's mouth twisted in disgust. "No. He was gone when I got there. Out the back door to his horse. I got a glimpse of him riding out of town."

"I'll get men together and follow."

Stroking his jaw, Griff shook his head. "He'll be long gone by the time we're ready to ride."

"You're certain it was Dugan?"

"Who else would be shooting at us?"

Redemption's Edge Ranch

Carrie folded the last piece of clothing, setting it in her satchel with the rest of her belongings. She'd had a restless night, getting perhaps three hours of scattered sleep.

Griff's surprise announcement to end their courtship, and her worry over the most stubborn man she'd ever known, had her staring out the window or at the ceiling. It had taken a while after he left for the hurt to turn to anger, then to a steely determination.

His decision had freed her from any influence Griff held, including his desire she stay at the Pelletier ranch.

"Are you certain about going back to town? Griff made a good argument for you staying with us." Rachel moved from her spot at the door.

"I'm certain. There's no reason for me to stay."

"Because he ended the courtship?" Rachel's voice held a hint of disappointment.

Closing the satchel, Carrie leaned against the bed with a resigned sigh. "Yes. There's no reason for me to hide now that Griff and I won't be seeing each other." Walking to the window, she fingered the pendant around her neck. "I should also get back to work. Georgina will probably travel on to California, Doc Worthington is retiring, and Doc McCord has hired his replacement."

"A replacement? Who?" As Doc Worthington's niece, and a nurse herself, Rachel tried to keep up with any changes at the clinic.

"His name is Drake Ralston. He and Doc McCord knew each other during the war. It was a blessing to have him there when Morgan was shot. The two of them saved the deputy's life."

Joining Carrie at the window, Rachel stared out at the barn and corrals. "What's he like?"

"I'm not ready to make any decisions about him, but he seems competent. More so than some doctors I worked with in New York."

"Single?"

A brittle laugh burst from Carrie's throat. "Clay mentioned Drake is a widower."

"Children?"

"I don't know. The same as many people in Splendor, my sense is the doctor came here for a fresh start." Carrie's fingers were still on her pendant. She and Drake had something in common. Both of them were starting over.

"I'm taking you back to town, so you'll have to introduce me."

"You'll be returning to the ranch alone?"

"Dax left for town a while ago. We'll escort each other home." A mischievous smile lifted the corners of her mouth, then disappeared when she thought of the other reason for her to ride into town. "I want to visit Isabella. When Travis left the ranch, he didn't look happy."

"Griff wouldn't tell me the reason for his quick departure. I know it had something to do with a decision Isabella made."

"Then I must make sure she's all right. We can go there first if you want?"

Carrie had already decided she'd visit Isabella after unpacking. "I'd love to go with you."

Griff looked between Isabella and Travis, feeling a deep ache in the area of his chest. "Are you certain this is what both of you want?"

Travis stared at the floor in Gabe's parlor, his hands shaking. He didn't respond to the question. Opposite him,

Isabella's hands covered her stomach, her features stoic. She'd made up her mind, not allowing Travis to sway her.

"Yes, I'm certain."

At her words, Travis rose. Without acknowledging either Isabella or Griff, he made his way out of the room. Shoulders slumped, hands still trembling at his sides, his head never rose from staring at the floor. Griff didn't believe he'd ever seen a man in such extreme pain. Hearing the front door open, then close, he turned toward Isabella.

"I don't understand why you'd rather end your marriage than take Travis back. You love each other, anyone can see it when you're together. And he wants the baby."

"Because I threatened a divorce."

"Which we both know is why you had me deliver the message to him. You wanted him to know the desperation you felt. His reaction was what you wanted, Isabella. Why would you now insist on the divorce?"

"He doesn't want the baby."

"That's not what he said. You know the opposite is true."

"Travis said what I wanted to hear."

"I disagree. He said what was in his heart." Griff leaned back in his chair, steepling his fingers under his chin.

"I...I..." Covering her face with both hands, she rocked back and forth.

Softening his voice, he tried again. "Has he ever lied to you?"

Dropping her hands, she shook her head. "Never."

"Yet you're convinced what he told you today wasn't the truth."

A knock at the door had both glancing toward the front.

"I'll get it." Rising from his chair, Griff found himself hoping to find Travis standing on the porch. Pulling the door open, his jaw dropped. After a quick acknowledgment of Rachel, his angry gaze locked on Carrie. "What the hell are you doing here?"

Chapter Twenty-One

Stepping in front of a speechless Carrie, planting fisted hands on her hips, Rachel glared at Griff. "That is quite enough. We're here to see Isabella. Why are *you* here?"

Blowing out a long breath, he stepped onto the porch, closing the door behind him. "Isabella asked me here."

"What about?"

"I'm sorry, Rachel. I can't share the reason with you. I can let you know Travis was here."

"We passed him on the trail from town. He rode on without looking at us. I've never seen him so devastated."

Opening the door, he motioned for Rachel to go inside. "Isabella is in the parlor. I'm sure she'd welcome your company." When Carrie tried to follow Rachel, Griff blocked her path. His attempt to control the anger in his voice failed.

"Why did you leave the ranch?"

Crossing her arms, she lifted her chin, fury choking her. "Because there's no longer a reason to stay."

"Dugan is still out there."

"He's after you, not me."

"As long as he believes you're important to me, you're as much a target as me."

"Within a couple days, everyone in town will know I'm no longer important to you. Problem solved." When she tried to step around him, he crossed his arms, filling the doorway. "Get out of my way."

"I know we're no longer seeing each other, Carrie. It doesn't mean you're not important to me."

"Hogwash. I doubt you ever cared about me. You gave me up too easily to have any feelings whatsoever. Now, let me pass." Stepping closer, she found herself blocked by an immovable wall of man. "I'm warning you, Griffin. Step aside."

"If I don't?"

She moved so fast he had no time to react. Drawing her foot back, she kicked him in the knee, causing him to buckle. Rushing around him, the curses spewing from his mouth could be heard in the parlor.

Isabella met her partway. "What happened?"

Glancing behind her, Carrie shrugged. "He tripped on my...boot." Hearing heavy footfalls, she hugged Isabella before joining Rachel on the sofa.

"What did you do?"

Carrie shrugged in answer to Rachel's question. "Nothing really."

Entering the parlor, Griff's face was a glowering mask of rage. "This conversation isn't over."

"It most certainly is. Now, if you'll excuse us, we want to talk to Isabella." When he didn't respond, she clarified. "In private."

He tore his gaze away from Carrie when Isabella placed a hand on his arm. "I'll come to your office in the morning, Griff."

Features softening, he gave a curt nod. "Please think about your decision, Isabella. I don't want you to have regrets later."

"I promise to give it a lot more thought. Does ten in the morning suit you?"

"Ten is fine." He shot Carrie a cold look. "Ladies."

When the front door closed, Isabella sat next to Carrie. "Did you and Griff have a fight?"

The anger in her voice gave way to unhidden misery. "No. We didn't fight."

"I don't understand."

"Griff ended our courtship."

Isabella stiffened, voice rising. "He didn't."

"Last night, he told me I wasn't what he wanted. It was a bit of a shock." Blinking her eyes, she tried to stop the tears threatening to fall. She was so tired of crying over Griff.

Isabella reached out, placing a hand on Carrie's arm. "He was lying."

Swiping away a lone tear, she didn't look up. "No, he wasn't. Griff doesn't believe I'm strong enough for a life out west."

Isabella swiped a hand through the air. "Rubbish. You're one of the strongest women I know."

Rachel stood, walking to the cabinet to pour a small amount of sherry for each of them. "He's afraid of losing you, Carrie." Handing a glass to the others, she sat back down, taking a slow sip.

"I'm sorry, but that doesn't make sense. He lost me by ending the courtship." She shifted toward Isabella. "Enough about my non-existent relationship with Griff. What happened with you and Travis?"

Swallowing the contents of her glass, Isabella walked to the cabinet, filling it again. Drinking it down, she poured another.

Rachel hurried over, taking the decanter from her hand. "Um...Isabella. Perhaps you should slow down."

"I'm afraid I made a huge mistake." She finished her third drink, stumbling a little before dropping onto the sofa. "He wanted to come home. I told him no."

Rachel's brows lifted. "You didn't."

Groaning, Isabella covered her face with her hands. "I thought he was telling me what I wanted to hear. I'd convinced myself Travis would never want the baby. Now, well...I'm not so sure."

"I've never known Travis to lie. I've always thought he wasn't capable of being dishonest."

A humorless chuckle bubbled up. "He's the most honest man I know, Rachel." Closing her eyes, Isabella grimaced. "I don't want to lose him."

"You won't," Rachel assured her. "You need to talk to him. Tell him what you told us. You're close to five months along. Everyone knows women with child don't always think clearly. Dax didn't ask me anything too important when I reached five months. Smart man."

Loud pounding had Rachel rushing to the door. Pulling it open, expecting to see Travis, she stilled. Two of

Gabe's deputies stood on the porch, Caleb Covington and Cash Coulter. They removed their hats.

"Caleb. Cash. No one is home except for Isabella, Carrie Galloway, and me."

Cash spoke first. "We'd like to speak with Isabella."

"Of course. Please come in. She's in the parlor." Rachel walked ahead of them, knowing both men knew the house almost as well as she did. "Isabella, Cash and Caleb need to speak with you."

Turning away to wipe away any moisture on her face, she stood, waiting as they approached. "Hello, Cash, Caleb. Would you like coffee or..." Her voice trailed off when Cash held up his hand.

"We need your help. Travis has been drinking for hours and won't leave the Dixie. I'm not sure he could walk out at this point. We don't want to take him to jail. We thought if you could talk to him, he might go home with you."

"Let me get my coat and hat."

Rachel picked up her own coat. "I'll come with you, Isabella."

"So will I." Carrie rushed to grab what she needed.

"We brought a wagon." Caleb helped Isabella into her coat. He looked at Rachel and Carrie. "Are you ladies going?"

Rachel nodded. "If there's room in the wagon."

"You'll need to bring blankets. I only brought one."

"I'll get them." Isabella rushed down a hall, tugging out three blankets. One each for Rachel and Carrie, and the third for Travis, assuming he'd listen to her through his drunken stupor.

It took little time to arrive at the Dixie. At noon, the bar was less than half full. Travis sat sprawled out in a chair, a bottle and glass on a nearby table. Gabe and Nick Barnett, the owners of the Dixie, sat with him. Griff stood a couple feet away, ready to help if needed.

Spotting the women, Gabe met them at the entrance. "Thanks for coming, Isabella."

A sadness washed over her at the sight of her husband. He rarely drank, and she'd never seen him drunk.

"He's real volatile. It took three of us to contain him during his last outburst."

Brows lifting, Isabella spoke to Gabe, keeping her gaze on Travis. "The last outburst?"

Chuckling, Gabe crossed his arms. "There've been three since I got here. He's angry and drunk, and as strong as a bull. None of us expected him to erupt as he did. I've never seen him in this state."

Isabella took a step forward, stopping when Gabe set a hand on her shoulder. "I'll go first. Nick and I can pretty much hold him back, but Griff is here if we need him." Gabe nodded to where Griff leaned against a nearby wall. He wasn't looking at Travis. Instead, his attention locked on Carrie.

Isabella waited until Gabe took a seat, her heart catching when Travis downed another drink. Whiskey, she assumed. Lowering herself into a chair, she leaned toward him, choking at the intense smell of alcohol.

"Travis?"

His eyes opened to slits. "What do you want?"

"I'm here to take you home."

"Go away, Izzy."

"Not unless you go with me."

Gripping the empty bottle, Travis tipped it toward his glass, surprised when nothing came out. Waving it in the air, he shifted in his chair. "Bartender. Another bottle."

Gabe, Nick, and Isabella shook their heads. Amos Henderson, the former owner of the Wild Rose, gave a nod of understanding.

"Travis, we need to go home. Are you hungry?"

"Hell no, I'm not hungry. I'm thirsty. Bartender!" He raised the bottle into the air a second time. "I'm empty."

Other than a tight grin, Amos didn't react.

Moving closer, Isabella touched his arm. "Come home with me, Travis. I'll fix you something to eat, then you can sleep for a while."

Shoving back his chair, Travis tried to stand. Unable to balance, he gripped the edge of the table before dropping back into the chair.

"Go away, Izzy."

"I can't."

Leaning toward her, he got within a few inches of her face. "I don't want you here."

"I'm not leaving unless you come with me."

Resting his arms on the table, he didn't meet her worried gaze.

"Travis?"

Finding it hard to lift his head, he stared at the scarred table. "Go away. Don't worry about me anymore. You have the baby. I can take care of myself."

Closing her eyes, Isabella felt the weight of her decision to obtain a divorce. She'd spoken out of hurt and anger. Seeing Travis now, defeated and alone, she knew it had been wrong.

"I can't sleep without you, Travis. Please, let's go home." Reaching out, she threaded her fingers through his.

"Home?"

"Yes. Home."

After a moment, he raised his head, his haggard expression piercing through her. "All right."

Chapter Twenty-Two

Carrie breathed a relieved sigh when Travis agreed to go home. While the men loaded him into the back of the wagon, she found herself watching Griff. He'd helped Isabella into the back of the wagon next to Travis. When she tucked blankets around both of them, he stepped back onto the boardwalk.

Carrie still didn't move from her spot outside the saloon. Not sure what she hoped to accomplish, she waited to see if Griff would join her. He didn't.

Checking his pocket watch, he looked up into a bright, clear sky. Hoping he'd acknowledge her in some way, she stayed in place, hands clasped in front of her. Carrie's heart pounded in a relentless beat as she waited for what he might do next.

She reminded herself he'd ended their courtship, no longer held an interest in her. Lying in bed last night, she'd convinced herself he'd done it to keep her safe. Perhaps she'd been wrong. The notion brought an unexpected emptiness, a tightness to her chest, and sharp pain to her heart.

A part of her knew she should leave, accept his decision and forget about him. Twice, she'd been wrong about a man's interest in her. First with Shane, and now with Griff. Maybe love and family weren't in her future.

Sensing movement, she looked up to see Griff had turned toward her. His features were blank, giving nothing away. Except for his piercing, gray eyes, which were cold as a winter storm. She wondered what he was thinking. Instead of asking, she straightened her back, lifted her chin, and walked past him.

He said nothing, letting her pass as if they'd never harbored feelings for each other. Perhaps he hadn't, and his attentions were nothing more than a way to fill his time, ease his loneliness. She found those thoughts too depressing to dwell on.

Rachel waited outside the newspaper office for Caleb to return with the wagon. Carrie joined her, saying nothing as her mind wrestled with Griff's decision to stop seeing her.

"Are you all right?"

Rachel's question didn't surprise Carrie. Her friend knew of her deep feelings for Griff.

"I'm fine. Or I will be in a few days. I'll go back to the clinic and return to life before Griff. You know, it's only been a few weeks since he showed an interest in me."

"Much can happen in a short period of time, Carrie. People have fallen in love in a few days."

"I may have. Not Griff. His defection hurts, is humiliating, but isn't life threatening."

Seeing Caleb maneuver the wagon toward them, both fell silent. They returned to Gabe and Lena's, thanked Caleb, and climbed into Rachel's wagon.

"I'll take you home, then I'm going to stop at the clinic to meet the new doctor. What's his name again?"

"Drake Ralston. You'll like him." Carrie recalled her first impression of the doctor. Tall and wiry, with an easy smile, sandy brown hair, and penetrating brown eyes with gold flecks. Sadness surrounded him, and she wondered how long it had been since he'd lost his wife.

The house was empty and quiet. Not unusual during the day, as both she and Georgina were usually at the clinic. Carrie emptied her satchel before starting a pot of coffee. Her stomach rumbled, reminding her she hadn't eaten for several hours.

Opening the back door, she saw a large, covered pot wedged between several pieces of firewood. In the winter, they often left food outside to keep it cold. Lifting the pot, she carried it inside, lifted the lid, and groaned. Georgina's stew.

Before tasting it, Carrie knew it would be salty and bland. Covering it, she set it back outside. Searching the cupboards, she pulled down a tin of biscuits and a pot of berry preserves. Along with coffee, she'd have more than enough to satisfy her hunger.

Warming a biscuit in the skillet, she slathered it with preserves, and poured a cup of coffee. Sitting down, she stared at the food, her appetite not as strong as earlier. The first bite tasted dry, without flavor. Tossing it aside, she picked up her cup. The coffee was better.

She took her cup into the living room, more than ready to stretch out, close her eyes, and forget the last twenty-four hours. Propping her feet on the table in front of the sofa, she shoved thoughts of Griff, and what may have been, aside.

Carrie would be back in the clinic tomorrow, back to her usual schedule, and around people she trusted. It would be a good long time before she was ready to even consider getting close to another man.

She didn't know how much time had passed before a knock on the front door had her eyes opening. Placing her hands over her ears, she tried to return to sleep. The knocking resumed, forcing her to answer the door.

Plodding to the door, she drew it open, and stilled.

"Hello, Carrie. May I come in?"

She stared at Griff. "What for?"

"I want to explain about last night."

Too tired to listen to his excuses about why he no longer had an interest in her, she began to close the door.

"Carrie, wait."

"I don't think so, Griff. Goodbye."

Putting his hand out, he stopped her from locking him out. "I'm asking for ten minutes."

"Truly, there's no need to explain your reasons. They're no longer important to me."

A long silence passed between them before Griff blew out a resigned breath. "All right, Carrie. I won't bother you again."

She stood at the open doorway, watching his retreating back. Leaning against the jamb, she had to stop the urge to call Griff back, give him the ten minutes he asked for. What good would it do except result in another night without sleep?

The clock on the wall showed four in the afternoon. Too early for bed and too late for a couple of quick errands. Closing the door, she took one more look into the distance, disappointment crushing her. Of course Griff wouldn't still be outside, she'd watched him walk away.

Without warning, one tear, then another, and another leaked from her eyes. They streamed down her cheeks until it felt as if a dam had broken and couldn't be plugged.

Closing the door to her bedroom, she fell back on the bed, placing an arm over her eyes. Had she been too quick to turn Griff away? Did he deserve ten minutes to explain himself?

"No." The word came out unbidden. Firm and unwavering. She would've smiled at herself if his rejection wasn't so fresh and painful.

She wished he'd made his reasons clear. A mirthless chuckle escaped. He'd tried to explain a few minutes ago, but she'd turned him away. Carrie couldn't help but think she'd made a grave mistake.

Griff wanted a drink. Several, actually. If he poured whiskey, it would be in the privacy of his office. Or his home. What a fool he'd been.

He'd spoken before thinking the other night at the Pelletiers'. Griff had feared for Carrie's life since the first bullet had pierced the evening air, missing them by inches.

"Missing," he muttered to himself and frowned. The Dave Dugan he knew wouldn't have missed such an easy shot. "Missed..." The word hung in the air. If Dugan wanted him or Carrie dead, they'd be laid out six feet under.

The night Morgan had been escorting Carrie home, and taken a bullet, bothered him. Dirty Dave would've recognized the deputy wasn't Griff. If not Dave, then who?

He found himself stopping in front of Ruby's Palace. Griff no longer craved a drink. Answers are what he sought. Not much got past Ruby Walsh.

Pushing open the heavy door, he stepped into a cavernous room cloaked in darkness. In another three hours, there'd be few tables left. Squinting, he spotted Ruby in deep conversation with the bartender. At the man's nod, she straightened, smiled, and walked toward him.

"Griffin MacKenzie. It's been too long."

"You look beautiful, as always." He pecked her cheek, inhaling the familiar scent of rose water.

"Such a charmer." She signaled to the bartender for two whiskeys. "I've heard you're courting the lovely nurse at the clinic. Carrie Galloway?" She sat down at a table, motioning for Griff to join her.

"For a time."

"Not any longer?"

He thanked the bartender for the drink, sipped the whiskey, then shook his head. "No, not any longer." Griff didn't want to talk about how he'd hurt a wonderful woman and ended a future he desperately wanted.

"You know Gabe has been looking for a man named Dave Dugan."

Ruby gave an almost imperceptible nod. "Dirty Dave is an odd character."

Griff raised one brow. "You know him?"

"Heard stories. Has Gabe found him?"

"Not yet. We're closer now that Dahlia drew an image of him without his beard and mustache."

"Gabe showed it to me. I wish I'd been able to help." Ruby finished her whiskey, setting the glass on the table. "That isn't why you came here, is it?"

"I'm the one who shot and killed Dugan's brother. It happened years ago in Texas. I believe that's why he's here in Splendor."

"I've heard about the shootings, and Deputy Wheeler."

"Have you noticed any other strangers in Splendor who've been around a while?"

"There are always men riding through town. Too many to remember, Griff. Can you be more specific?"

"Wish I could. I'm following my instincts on this, Ruby."

"And they tell you?"

"That Dugan may not be the shooter." Pushing away from the table, Griff stood. "Thanks, Ruby." Dropping money on the table, he walked out into an early evening, and the beginnings of another storm.

Ignoring the desire to go back to Carrie's house, try to talk her into seeing him, he walked straight to the jail. Griff had nothing to support his suspicions of a different shooter. He'd explain his reasoning to Gabe, and let the sheriff determine what to do.

Lost in his thoughts, Griff didn't see the woman come around a corner. He did feel her clip his shoulder. Reaching out, he grabbed her arm, steadying her before she fell to the ground.

"Are you all right?" Griff stared into deep blue eyes glowing with laughter.

Straightening her hat, she smiled. "Yes, I'm fine. Thank you for not letting me land in the icy mudhole."

Griff glanced beside them at a pool of ice and mud at least two feet in diameter. "I wouldn't have let that happen. I'm Griffin MacKenzie."

"Miss Helena Watson. It's a pleasure, Mr. MacKenzie."

"The pleasure is mine. May I escort you somewhere?"

"Thank you, but it's not necessary. I'm only going to the general store, then back to the hotel."

"At least allow me to escort you to Petermann's." Offering his arm, she slipped hers through it.

"Are you new to Splendor?"

"Quite. I arrived yesterday. It's a lovely town."

"On your way to?"

"San Francisco. I've decided to stay here a few more days, though. It's been a long trip."

"Where did your journey begin?"

"Baltimore. Do you live in Splendor?"

"For a couple years now."

"Then you must like it."

"Very much. I don't foresee leaving for a long time. Perhaps never."

She was quiet for a while, seeming to consider his words. "Someday, I'll find my own Splendor. For now, I'm happy traveling about, meeting new people such as yourself."

Griff slowed his pace as they approached the general store. "Here you are. I hope you have a memorable trip, Miss Watson."

"So do I, Mr. MacKenzie."

He waited on the boardwalk until she was inside. Turning, she flashed him a brilliant smile, waving goodbye through the window.

Helena Watson was a beautiful woman with startling blue eyes, golden blonde hair, lush lips, and curves which would attract the attention of any man. Any man except Griff.

No matter her heart-stopping beauty, she wasn't Carrie. He doubted any woman could come close to the lovely lady who held his heart. All he had to do now was convince her to give him another chance.

Chapter Twenty-Three

Carrie contemplated what to do next. Georgina arrived not long before supper was ready, announcing she'd made the decision to leave Splendor by the middle of March. No matter how Carrie phrased a response, her friend and fellow nurse refused to be dissuaded. Notice had already been given to Dr. McCord, who would pass it on to Dr. Worthington. If they found someone to replace her earlier, she'd be on the next stage out of town.

While hating the decision, Carrie understood. Georgina had spoken of San Francisco often, intending to travel there before settling down. Most times, she'd encourage Carrie to join her. This was the first time she'd considered going.

She'd been courted twice since arriving in Splendor. The first had ended when Shane backed away to court the woman he'd loved most of his life. The second because...well, she didn't understand why Griff walked away. Probably never would. People characterized women as fickle. From Carrie's experience, it had been the men who'd changed their minds. She didn't begrudge either man, but her desire to stay diminished with each disappointment.

Unlike Georgina, Carrie wouldn't leave until the doctors had found suitable replacements. Which could take months. Regardless of her decision, Carrie didn't see herself leaving Splendor for a long time.

Switching her gaze between the cooling cup of coffee before her, and the street outside her living room, she thought of ways to occupy her time when not at the clinic.

She'd heard Ruby Walsh had been hinting at starting a repertory company to perform for the townsfolk. Far different from the performances at the Palace, the company would be made of talented citizens who could sing, dance, or play music.

Before leaving New York, Carrie had been part of such a group. They'd performed at a neighborhood church to audiences between ten and fifty. She could sing and dance well enough to be selected, but didn't have the talent for professional shows. It had been fun and rewarding.

The reverend's wife, Ruth Paige, had spoken about enlarging the library at the church. Gabe and Nick had volunteered a larger space at no cost. To move forward, she needed people to solicit books, and volunteer librarians. Carrie could certainly be one of the volunteers.

Then there was Rachel, who'd been inviting Carrie to visit for several days so they could ride together. She liked the idea, a way to get out of town and away from those she'd rather not run into.

Another thought hit her. When Georgina left, there'd be no one to share expenses. Carrie couldn't afford the house by herself. She'd need a new roommate or be forced to find a room somewhere. Suzanne's boardinghouse was almost always full, which meant Carrie would be looking for a room in a private residence.

The only place she knew about with a room always available was in Gladys Poe's house. She couldn't imagine living with the town gossip. Even the thought depressed her.

Telling herself it would all work out, she refilled her cup, stirring in a small amount of sugar. Sitting back down, Carrie glanced out the window in time to see Griff walking past her house to his. The sight of him caused her heart to squeeze. Without much thought, she closed the curtains. If she couldn't see him, he couldn't be there, right? A ridiculous notion, but one she could make herself believe.

Less confident than earlier, she dumped her coffee down the sink and grabbed her coat. Slipping it on, she stepped outside. A light snow fell, not enough to discourage her from a short walk.

Wrapping a wool scarf around her neck, Carrie set out in the opposite direction of Griff's house. No need to pick at a wound that hadn't healed.

There were still some lamps on in several shops. Music from Ruby's Palace spilled onto the street, a toe-tapping song she'd never heard before. If she'd still been with Griff, Carrie would've dragged him inside to dance. A soft chuckle escaped before she drew her mouth into a firm line. Griff didn't deserve to be in her thoughts.

Continuing to Frontier Street, she hesitated, watching a small crowd gather outside the Dixie. Carrie would seldom be drawn to one of the saloons. Something about the way the men mingled in small groups, mumbled among themselves, had her curious.

Careful to avoid the numerous ruts of mud and ice, Carrie made her way across the street. A booming voice, powerful and crisp, had people shoving to get inside the Dixie. She didn't recognize the deep, commanding sound that silenced the crowd.

Stepping between two men, she tried to spot the reason for so many standing outside on a frigid night. She couldn't. What she did see had her backing away.

Griff stood inside, arms crossed, a steady gaze on someone. She guessed him to be the man who had the crowd mesmerized. Carrie didn't want to leave before taking a look at the person speaking, and listening to what others found captivating. She'd have to be careful. Having Griff see her would be awkward and painful.

Scooting behind several people, she stopped several feet away from Griff. His back was to her, his gaze intent on the speaker. Comfortable in her position, she began listening to the story the man told about a gunfighter, a lady, and a murder.

The detail was such she could picture the scenes he described. When he got to the part where the gunfighter shot the lady, using popping noises to emphasize the gun firing, she flinched. Others around her did the same. Griff didn't show any reaction.

Inching to the right, she got her first glimpse of the man. Carrie couldn't tell his height. He tended toward the heavier side, had bright red hair, and graying handlebar mustache and beard. What caught her attention was the man's unsettling gray eyes.

They held an eerie glow, as she'd seen in an image of a wolf. She and a few friends had visited a gallery in New York showing an exhibit of animals, domesticated and wild. The wolf had captivated her. Carrie had stared at it so long her friends had to drag her away for their supper engagement.

So focused on the speaker, and his unnerving eyes, she didn't notice Griff watching her until the crowd parted, allowing a man to leave the saloon. Shifting to allow him to pass, her gaze slammed into Griff's. He didn't look away, nor did he try to get closer.

The pain of the future she'd lost had her stepping away. Inching back, she didn't notice the edge of the boardwalk until a foot slipped off. Arms flailing, she tried to right herself, knowing it was too late to stop the expected outcome.

An instant before the point where she'd land in the muddy snow, strong hands grabbed her. Griff set her on the plank walkway, waiting for Carrie to regain her balance. Their eyes met again for a second before she felt her face heat and moved away.

"Thank you."

Griff closed the distance without touching her. "I'm surprised you're here."

He was too close, his nearness suffocating. Edging away again, she shrugged. "I was curious about the crowd."

"It's Judge Hoodoo Hardin. He's an excellent storyteller. He also has no compassion for anyone who's broken the law."

Again, she took a couple small steps away. "I've never seen him before."

Nodding toward the inside of the Dixie, he moved toward her. "He rode in a few days ago."

"Oh." Glancing over her shoulder, her chin jutted toward Griff. "I'd better go."

"I'll walk you home, Carrie."

She shook her head. "No. I'm used to getting home by myself. Enjoy your evening." Whirling about, Carrie hurried along the boardwalk, putting distance between them. A hundred steps away, she felt his hand on her shoulder.

"Carrie, slow down."

Shaking off his hand, she glared at him. "I'm perfectly capable of getting home by myself. Besides, you don't want the shooter to see us together."

Griff winced at the censure combined with disillusionment in her voice. It hurt to see what he'd caused by his impulsive act to walk away.

"I've been a fool, Carrie."

"I won't argue the point." She lifted her skirt, preparing to cross the street. He took her arm, holding her back.

"I shouldn't have ended our courtship."

"Well, you did. Now, please, let me go."

"Let me explain, Carrie. It won't take long."

"It won't take any time because I don't care about your explanation. You wanted me out of your life, and I'm doing my best to make it easy on you. On both of us."

He scrubbed a hand over his face, exhausted and frustrated. "I don't want easy. What I want is to forget the other night and go on as we were."

"You're out of your mind. Everything changed when you rode away from the Pelletier ranch."

"I made a mistake, and for that, I'm sorry, Carrie."

Brows drawing together, her mouth twisted. "Mistake? You called off our courtship, and now you're telling me it was a mistake?"

"Yes. Men do make mistakes, you know."

Feeling tired, and confused, she walked to a nearby bench and sat down. "All right. Say what you need to so I can go home."

Joining her, he bent forward, resting his arms on his thighs. He wondered where to start, deciding to tell her a story.

"Years ago, one of my closest friends married a woman from Boston, and brought her to his house in Austin. He'd been a Texas Ranger for several years, made enough enemies to last a lifetime. She was a bright woman, trained to run a household and take care of the children.

"When his past caught up with him, putting his life in danger, his wife had no skills to deal with the danger. She packed her belongings and returned to her *safe* life in Boston."

Carrie stiffened at the analogy, understanding Griff saw her as fragile, incapable of facing a threat to him or her. He'd judged and found her guilty without knowing anything about her past.

"Let me guess. She was killed in Boston during a robbery."

Gaze flying to hers, he nodded. "A bank robbery. She took a bullet to the heart."

Grimacing, she felt awful for the woman and Griff's friend. "I'm not like her."

Standing, he paced several feet away, staring across the street at nothing in particular. "No, you aren't. You're a strong woman, Carrie. The other night, I forgot how capable you are, and let my fear of losing you control my thoughts. And my words."

Facing her, he held out both hands, palms up. "I'm asking you to forgive me. Allow us to start again."

Carrie's gaze moved from his hands to his face, seeing the apology in his eyes. She hadn't been prepared for the deep hurt his calling off their courtship caused. Hadn't realized how deep her love for him had grown. Walking to him, she gripped his hands in hers.

"There's nothing to forgive. I'm glad you shared the story with me. It makes it easier to understand why you acted as you did."

"And starting over?"

Her hesitation surprised Carrie. She understood the cause. Fear he'd do it again. "May I have time to think about it?"

Disappointment flashed in his eyes before he concealed it. "You can take as long as you need. I'll wait for you, Carrie. Now, may I escort you home?"

Chapter Twenty-Four

Isabella placed a cold cloth over Travis's forehead before moving to the window to draw the curtains tight, keeping the early morning sun from landing on the bed. As she'd expected, her husband had a restless night, saying her name more than once in his sleep.

Once he awoke, Travis would face a horrible day. For a man who almost never drank, two bottles were going to cause a great deal of hurt. A glass of water and packets of headache medicine were already on the bed table.

Leaving long enough to take care of her morning needs, she returned to find Travis trying to get out of bed. Releasing a tired breath, she hurried to him.

"What do you think you're doing?" She tried to press him back down, but he waved her away.

"Go away, Isabella."

"Not until you tell me where you're going."

"To the ranch. I have work to do." Attempting to stand, his head spun, and he sat back down. "My head's exploding."

She crossed her arms. "Two bottles of whiskey will do that to a man."

His bloodshot eyes focused on her. "Why are you here?" He pressed fingers to his temples, wincing. "You want a divorce, fine. I'll sign whatever you want."

A thudding pain clamped around her heart. "We'll talk when you're better."

"I'm fine now. So talk." He waved a hand in the air, then wished he hadn't when his stomach churned.

Travis reached for the packet of headache medicine and the glass of water. Isabella watched as his hands shook, causing some water to spill onto his lap. She didn't offer her help.

When finished taking the medicine and emptying the glass, he lifted an accusing gaze to hers. "You want a divorce. I agreed. There's nothing to talk about. It would be best if you left me alone."

The venom in his voice had her taking a step away. Wrapping her arms around her waist, she forced herself to get her thoughts out. "There are issues to discuss, Travis. The talk can wait until you feel better."

Closing his eyes, he gave a derisive snort. "Do whatever you want. You have plenty of money to raise the baby alone. You've never needed me, Isabella, and you sure as hell don't need me now."

Anger at his words flared. She took several steps to stand by the bed. "This is *our* baby, Travis. Yours and mine. Yes, I have money. You've known about my wealth since well before we married. So, I have to believe this isn't about money. It's about the child. The one you don't want."

Exhausted and hurting more than he had in years, his eyes opened to slits. "I never said I didn't want the baby, Isabella. You're the one who grew impatient and made a decision that will separate us permanently."

The color drained from her face. She reached out to grasp the edge of the wardrobe, steadying herself. He'd told the truth. She had grown impatient from missing her husband and fearing he'd never return. Hearing Travis say it aloud emphasized how her decision would ruin a relationship she treasured above all others. Her voice lowered to a whisper.

"I love you, Travis. A divorce isn't what I want."

A tired sigh escaped. "Then what do you want?"

"For us to raise our child together."

The silence stretched on for a long time before Travis answered. "I want the same."

A tear fell, then another, before Isabella offered a tentative smile, and broke down in relieved sobs.

Griff and Carrie stood on the stoop of her house, both hesitant to end their time together. They knew Carrie had a decision to make. One which would signal a possible future together, or end whatever had started.

Griff knew the decision would depend on trust. Carrie had forgiven him for his impulsive decision. Could she trust he wouldn't walk away as he had before? Believe that he'd give them a chance at a future?

"May I come by tomorrow to escort you to supper?"

A hint of sadness washed over her face. "I'm having supper with Georgina. She's leaving for San Francisco as soon as the doctors find a replacement. Frannie, Rose, and Amy are joining us."

"Has she tried to talk you into going with her?" Griff hoped not.

"You know she has."

Carrie was right. He never doubted Georgina's persistence at talking her friend into leaving with her.

"Are you considering it?"

"No. Splendor is where I want to be. My work is rewording, I have friends here, and there's a man I'm quite fond of." She offered a cautious smile. There was so much to think about. "Someday, I would love to visit California. Now isn't the time."

Griff stroked a finger down her cheek, loving how soft she felt. "It's beautiful. The ocean is different from the Atlantic."

"You've been there?"

"The MacLaren ranch is inland from San Francisco. I've been to the city many times. Someday, perhaps you'll allow me to take you there."

Carrie wanted to say yes, but couldn't quite get the word out. She believed Griff's reasons for his rash decision, his strong desire to start again. The problem was the hurt still lingered. The knot in her stomach had yet to fade. Her heart urged her to start over with the man she loved. It was her mind holding her back.

"Maybe."

The sound of someone running toward them had Griff shoving open her door and lifting her inside. Closing the door as he drew his gun, he watched through a window. Seconds passed before a boy of perhaps twelve ran past the house, another boy on his heels. Holstering his gun, Griff stood.

"Just a couple of boys chasing each other."

Turning, he stilled at the sight of Carrie. She'd lost all color, as if she were about to pass out. One hand pressed against her chest. He wrapped her in his arms.

"It's all right, sweetheart."

"I know." She laced fingers behind his back, her head resting on his chest. Although both wore heavy coats, she could feel heat pass between them. Holding him felt good. Even if it had been just a couple days, she'd missed this. "I'm fine, really. It was a surprise is all."

Leaning back, he studied her face, seeing the color return. Kissing the top of her head, he dropped his arms and stepped away.

"I should let you get ready for bed." As he said it, the door to Georgina's bedroom opened a crack.

"Is that you, Carrie?"

"Me and Griff."

"Oh." He heard surprise in her voice.

"I'm just leaving." Lowering his voice, Griff kissed Carrie's cheek before moving to the door. "Save Saturday for me. If the weather is good, we'll take a ride."

Three days away. She'd hoped to see him sooner, but decided to keep that to herself. "I'd love to go. Should I pack lunch?"

"If it isn't too much trouble."

"Not at all."

Again, he hesitated, not ready to leave, knowing he had to get out of there. "I'll see you Saturday."

Closing the door behind him, she stood there for several minutes. The day had turned out differently than she'd anticipated. Much better than she could've hoped.

Leaving his office for lunch, he stepped into another beautiful day. Cold and clear, he found himself thinking of Saturday, hoping it would be as nice.

McCall's was busy with one table open. Nodding at Betts, he hung his coat on a hook as the door opened and the woman he'd met on the boardwalk entered. Her gaze moved over the room, seeing what Griff had. No tables. Then she saw him sitting alone at a table for four. A broad smile appeared as she closed the distance between them.

"Would it be too forward to ask if you want company?"

He struggled to recall her name. Then it came to him. "Hello, Miss Watson. Please do join me." Pulling out a chair, she flashed him another smile.

"You must call me Helena. May I call you Griffin?"

It surprised him that she remembered his name. "Griff."

"Griff it is."

Conversation came easy with Helena. She was well read, had traveled extensively, and knew many interesting people. Her stories made him laugh, which had been missing from his life since the first shot at Carrie's house.

The front door opened, and Griff felt an unbidden rush of guilt. Still wearing her nurse's uniform, she looked tired. He wondered if she'd gotten any sleep. The thought evaporated when her gaze landed on him. Lifting a hand to have her join them, a smile appeared on her face, then disappeared when she saw the woman at his table.

Griff saw the instant she made her decision. Instead of coming toward him, she turned away, and left.

"Excuse me, Helena." Leaving his coat, he hurried outside. Looking one way, then the other, he spotted her crossing the street toward the boardinghouse.

"Carrie! Carrie, wait."

Instead of stopping, she slowed her pace, entering the boardinghouse restaurant. He doubted her reaction would've been the same if they weren't already dealing with his idiotic decision to end their courtship. Carrie would've joined him and Helena, thinking nothing about it.

Already wary of him, she'd seen the worst. If their positions were reversed, he might've done the same.

Griff found her sitting alone at a table in a back corner. She didn't look up when he approached. Knowing he should return to McCall's, explain his absence to Helena, he chose to speak with Carrie.

"May I join you?"

There was no rancor in her eyes when she met his gaze. "I believe you already have a table at McCall's."

"There were no tables when she arrived. She asked about sharing my table. Her name is Helena Watson. You could've joined us." Pulling out a chair, he sat down.

"I didn't want to intrude. She could've been a client."

"She isn't. Helena is a woman who needed a table. Nothing more."

Carrie looked away before responding. "Go back to McCall's, Griff. Finish your lunch. I'll see you Saturday."

Suzanne set a bowl in front of Carrie. "Here you are. Chicken stew and biscuits. Griff, are you joining her?"

"Not today, Suzanne."

"Let me know if you change your mind."

Watching Carrie tuck into her lunch while ignoring him, he stood. "I'll be at your house at eleven on Saturday, Carrie."

Waiting until he left, she put down her spoon and sat back. She'd overreacted. Seeing him with a beautiful woman shouldn't have bothered her. Yet it did.

If she trusted him, believed in him as she had a few days ago, she would've thought the best instead of the worst. Carrie hated where they were. Not together, yet not apart.

Appetite gone, she set money on the table, slipped into her coat, and stepped back into a glorious day. When entering McCall's, she'd been in a wonderful mood, excited about Saturday.

Seeing Griff with Helena Watson triggered doubt. Carrie had a decision to make, and it had to be soon. Either she could trust him or she couldn't. They both deserved to move forward. Either with each other or on their own.

Chapter Twenty-Five

Griff read over the most recent changes to Isabella's will for the last time, finding nothing to cause concern. He'd been surprised when she and Travis had shown up late Thursday morning to discuss the modifications.

The fact they'd reconciled had been a pleasant surprise. The delicate part turned out to be a disagreement between the couple on Isabella's wishes. Travis had strong objections to adjusting the percentage. He argued the majority should still go to their child, with him receiving a much smaller amount.

In her quiet way, Isabella had explained her reasons three times before Travis agreed. Griff had answered questions, doing his best to stay out of the actual discussion. He'd known the outcome from the moment Travis objected to the changes. Given the extent of Isabella's wealth, he knew her wishes would prevail.

He checked the time. Almost ten on Friday morning. A few minutes remained before they returned to finalize the will.

Walking to the stove, he added wood before making a fresh pot of coffee. His thoughts shifted to Carrie, and her reaction to seeing him with Helena.

Griff hadn't known what to expect when he followed her to the boardinghouse. To his relief, she'd been calm, listened to his explanation, and still looked forward to Saturday. He hadn't seen or spoken to her since.

A knock on his door broke through his thoughts of Carrie. Thinking it was Isabella and Travis, he drew the door open, then stepped back.

"Judge Hardin. I wasn't expecting you."

The judge stuck out his hand. "Griffin MacKenzie. Never thought I'd see you again."

Accepting the offered hand, Griff stepped aside. "Please, come in. I'll warn you. I expect clients any minute."

Waving a hand in the air, the judge lowered himself into a chair. "Thought I saw you at the Dixie the other night."

"You had quite an audience. Can I get you some coffee?"

"No, no. This will only take a minute. Perhaps we can meet for supper before I leave town."

"Let me know when. Now, tell me what brings you here."

Several minutes later, Griff massaged the back of his neck, considering all the judge had told him. "I'm glad you came to warn me."

"I'll be honest, Griff. If I see Dugan first, you won't have to deal with him."

"You aren't thinking of going outside the law, are you?"

Standing, the judge picked up his hat. "Let's just say I have no intention of letting him ruin any more lives."

Griff didn't like the answer. He knew enough to understand Hoodoo Hardin would do whatever he wanted.

Walking to the door, the judge turned back. "Saturday night, Griff. Supper at the Eagle's Nest."

"May I bring a friend?"

"A woman?"

"Yes."

Laughing, the judge lifted his hand in farewell. "I'd be angry if you didn't."

Carrie pulled on the boots she'd purchased at the general store. They were made for a man, brown leather, and the smallest size Stan Petermann carried. Standing, she shoved her feet all the way inside before dropping her skirt. The extra thick wool socks Petermann suggested bunched under her toes and heels. She didn't let the slight discomfort bother her. The boots were still better than anything else she owned.

A quick look out the window showed a gorgeous day. The excitement of the upcoming ride was tempered by the conversation she knew Griff would expect.

There'd been no big change in her thinking. Carrie still had reservations about renewing their courtship. Even the remaining doubt didn't stop her from wanting to see him. She didn't believe anything would eliminate the deep longing she held for Griff. Carrie suspected her love for him was at fault.

Slipping into her coat, she walked into the living room at the soft knock on the front door. Letting out a long, shaky breath, she grabbed the handle.

"Good morning, Griff. Let me get my hat and I'll be ready to leave."

Taking tentative steps inside, he grinned at the sight of what she wore. "Nice boots."

Lifting her skirt, she grinned. "Do you like them?"

He pretended to think about his answer, before nodding. "They're quite fetching."

"Fetching, huh?"

"Much better for riding than your other shoes." Griff tilted his head at the boxy-looking hat she put on. "Next, you need a better hat."

"What's wrong with this one?"

"Other than it not protecting your face, neck, or ears?"

Entering her bedroom, Carrie stood in front of the mirror, studying the hat. "I suppose there are other hats that would be better."

An idea struck him. "If you're ready, let's get you on the horse."

Helping her mount, he adjusted the stirrups before swinging into his own saddle. Instead of heading out of town, Griff rode to Frontier Street, reining up in front of the general store.

"What are we doing?"

Raising his hands, he helped her to the ground, threading his fingers through hers. "We're buying you a proper hat to go with your proper boots."

The ride wasn't long, less than an hour from town. The temperature remained above freezing, with a bright sun and clear sky. They were on the brink of spring.

Carrie kept touching her new hat, a small grin appearing each time. Made of beaver, the brim was wide and floppy, protecting her face from the sun.

"It looks good on you."

Glancing at Griff, she sent him a grateful look. "You didn't need to buy it for me. I could've paid for it."

"I wanted to."

"Thank you, Griff. It's perfect."

They took a different trail than the one a couple weeks earlier. This one followed along a canyon rim. Across the open expanse, two waterfalls crashed down the face of the canyon, landing in a pool before joining a creek.

Carrie couldn't stop staring at the majestic sight. A few minutes later, they reached their destination.

Griff found a spot where the snow had melted to spread out a blanket. "Are you hungry?"

"Starving. What can I do?"

Reaching into his saddlebags, Griff pulled out two wrapped packages Carrie had given him. "You can take these to the blanket." Pulling out two more, he joined her at the blanket.

He unwrapped fried chicken with biscuits and jam, then opened the packages containing a bean salad and two slices of pie. "This is wonderful, Carrie."

They took their time, saying little, allowing themselves the quiet each sought. Both knew the conversation ahead wouldn't be easy.

Carrie had already decided to take their relationship a day at a time. No pressure, and no promises. She needed time to rebuild her trust in Griff, to believe she was who he wanted.

Finishing her second piece of chicken and a biscuit with a thick layer of jam, she leaned back, lifting her face to the sun. Closing her eyes, she didn't notice Griff watching, a slow grin spreading across his face. Reaching out, he tucked wayward strands of hair behind her ear.

He leaned down, meaning to brush his lips across hers when a shot rang through the quiet. *Rifle*, he thought, at the same time a bullet landed less than a foot from Carrie.

Drawing his six-shooter, Griff moved quickly to shield her with his body. "Stay down and don't move until I tell you."

The next bullet tore into the blanket by Griff's legs. Covering her, he lifted enough to look around, seeing nothing to help locate the shooter. Certain the bullets came from the north, he concentrated on the bushes about twenty yards away.

Another rifle shot tore a second hole in the blanket. Either the person was a bad shot, or the bullets were meant to pin them down. He couldn't begin to understand the reason.

"We need to find cover." When she didn't respond, he pushed on her shoulder. "Carrie."

"Yes." To his surprise, her voice held no hint of fear.

"See the trees to your left?"

Raising her head, she nodded. "Yes."

"That's where we're going. Ready?"

Reaching out, she grasped his free hand, and squeezed. "Ready."

Before Griff could move, a series of shots tore over their heads in the opposite direction. Not rifle shots. The bullets were from a six-shooter. Actually, two six-shooters by Griff's count.

Whoever owned the rifle responded. Within seconds, Carrie and Griff were caught in a gun battle between two opponents. Neither moved. There was no safe place to hide.

"What's happening, Griff?" This time, her voice trembled, confused and scared.

He spoke next to her ear. "I don't know. Just stay down and don't move. There's no place for us to go."

It had been a long time since he'd felt so helpless. Even with a revolver, he didn't know where to aim. Couldn't distinguish friend from foe.

Covering her body with his, Griff rested his cheek against hers. Instead of slowing, the number of bullets increased, some landing within inches of their prone bodies. It would be a miracle if they lived through the constant volley of bullets.

Believing their situation couldn't get worse, an earsplitting explosion came from a third location. A second blast erupted a moment later.

Griff recognized the sound as coming from a scattergun, a powerful weapon capable of blowing a hole the size of a saucer through a man's chest.

Covering her head with his hands, he tried to protect Carrie from the shot raining down on them. From what Griff could figure, the person with the six-shooters and owner of the scattergun were aiming for the same target. Unless the rifleman hightailed it out of there soon, he wouldn't have long to live.

A third, then a fourth blast blew past them toward the owner of the rifle at the same time another barrage of bullets flew from the revolvers. A scream, loud enough to waken the dead, sounded from behind them. The location Griff believed the person with the rifle hunkered down.

The area grew eerily silent. Smoke from the firearms hung in the air. The acrid smell of gun powder saturated their hair, skin, and clothing.

The rattling sound of a man close to death broke the silence. "Stay here, Carrie."

Griff pushed off her, bending down as he rushed toward the bushes to the north. Breaking through the thick growth, he came to a stop. Judge Hoodoo Hardin, a shotgun in his hand, and the woman he knew as Helena

Watson, stood over the man. At her waist was a pair of ivory handled six-shooters.

Glancing at the man Griff knew was moments from death, he recognized Dirty Dave Dugan.

Chapter Twenty-Six

Arms crossed, a shoulder leaning against a wall of the jail, Griff listened as Gabe questioned Judge Hardin and Helena Watson. She'd admitted it was an alias. Her real name turned out to be Trina O'Brien, a well-known bounty hunter.

Dugan's body had been taken to the undertaker's office. Filled with shot from the scattergun and half a dozen bullets from Trina's guns, it was a miracle Dugan lasted as long as he did. The four had ridden back to town together, Dirty Dave's body draped over the back of the judge's horse.

Through it all, Carrie had remained stoic, not flinching when she'd joined Griff, Hardin, and O'Brien as they watched Dugan take his last breath. She'd dropped to her knees, checking the outlaw's pulse. Glancing up, she'd shaken her head before looking at the time on the watch brooch pinned to her blouse.

Carrie refused to be left at her house while Griff met Gabe at the jail. The sheriff, flanked by deputies Jonas Taylor and Tucker Nolan, questioned the judge and Trina until he had a clear picture of what happened.

Griff verified if it hadn't been for them, he and Carrie wouldn't have made it back to town alive. Carrie concurred. As for the bounty on Dugan, Judge Hoodoo had no interest in the money. He'd relinquished any claim on the reward to Trina.

Settling his hat firmly on his head, Hoodoo slapped his hands on Gabe's desk and stood. "This has been an excellent day. The world is safe from another murderer. I'm going to the Dixie. You're all welcome to join me as my guests."

With a nod toward Griff and Carrie, he stalked outside, accompanied by Trina O'Brien. The bounty hunter had already announced she'd be leaving Splendor in the morning. Her next target was a group of four women suspected of robbing banks in the Dakotas, Montana, and Wyoming. The youngest of the four had recently been sprung from the Moosejaw jail, rejoining her sisters in crime.

Griff stood outside the jail, watching the woman he'd known as Helena Watson cross the street arm-and-arm with Hoodoo, chatting away as if they'd known each other for years. Next to him, Carrie waited until his attention shifted to her, but he remained silent.

She didn't know what bothered him. Something in his expression warned her to give him time. She needed time, also. They'd almost died by Dugan's gun. If Hoodoo and Trina hadn't shown up, their bodies would be the ones being prepared for burial.

"I'm going to walk home, Griff." Giving a slow nod, he slipped her arm through his. "You don't have to accompany me. The danger to us is over."

Not replying, he continued to walk toward the street both lived on. Reaching her house, he stayed beside her until stopping at the front door. As she slipped her arm from his, Carrie startled at the desolation in his gaze.

"What's wrong, Griff? You seem upset."

Watching her for a moment, he gave a slow shake of his head. "You could've died because of me."

"I could also die crossing the street. Two people were killed last year when one stepped in front of a wagon, and the other a rampaging horse." She cupped his cheek. "Anything can happen, Griff. Still, we're both here and we're alive."

He quieted a moment before responding. "I should've protected you."

"You covered me with your body. What more could you have done?"

Glancing away, he stared down the street as if searching for an answer to his questions. Leaning down, he brushed a kiss across her cheek. "Sleep well, Carrie."

Watching him walk down the steps and toward his house, she had a horrible feeling what bothered him didn't bode well for the two of them.

Three days had passed since Carrie had seen Griff. She missed him, but refused to let his absence worry her. She knew he blamed himself for putting them in a position where they could've been killed. Her opinion of what happened was different.

Griff couldn't have known Dugan would follow them into the mountains. As far as protecting her, he'd used his body as a shield. Carrie was certain not all men would've put their lives at risk to save another. He accepted a great deal of responsibility for actions out of his control. She'd already made up her mind to find him if he didn't come to her by that evening.

The clinic had been slow. A boy of eleven had fallen out of a barn loft, breaking his arm. A young mother had brought in her young daughter when a fever lingered for three days. Two men had brought in their friend, a fellow miner, who'd collapsed after finishing his last shift.

By the time the clinic closed, she'd read a complete dime novel about a frontiersman who'd killed an attacking grizzly with his bare hands. Sensational and entertaining, she'd enjoyed it immensely.

Slipping on her heavy coat and new, floppy brimmed hat, she said goodbye to Doctors McCord and Ralston. Drake fit in with the rest of the staff. His skills were exceptional, and his calm manner gained the confidence of their patients.

Heading into the cold, clear evening, she walked straight toward Griff's house. Knowing he might still be at his office, she sat down on the lone chair he kept on his porch. Pulling a wrapped package containing two slices of sweet bread, Carrie broke off a small piece, chewing slowly while considering what she planned to say when Griff arrived. She didn't know it would be hours before he arrived.

Griff tossed back a second whiskey as well as throwing down the cards in his hand. He'd played with partial interest, winning, then losing, then winning again for the last couple hours.

His thoughts were on Carrie. He missed her, knew it was cowardice keeping him away.

Putting her in danger had never been his intention. Griff had done all he could to prevent it, even ending their courtship. But he couldn't stay away.

A short trip into the mountains had almost gotten them killed. Forgiving himself remained out of reach. Pride turned out to be a troublesome shadow, following him every minute of each day. There was one outcome if he didn't overcome it. He'd lose Carrie.

"I'm done, gentlemen." Griff shoved back his chair, grabbed his coat, and headed out.

The temperature had dropped a great deal since he'd walked into the Dixie. Checking the time, he saw it was close to nine. Stopping in front of Carrie's darkened house, he debated whether to knock or move on.

Shoving hands into his pockets, Griff let out a breath, which turned to steam when it mixed with the freezing air. Convincing himself she needed her sleep, knowing he wasn't quite ready to face her, he turned toward his house.

Closing in on his porch, his gaze locked on a bundled figure in his chair. Arms were wrapped around the person's waist, legs drawn up under the body.

Drawing the six-shooter, Griff slowed his pace, trying to identify who'd invaded his private space. Then his gaze locked on the floppy hat. Slamming the gun into the holster, he ran, closing the distance in a few steps. Dropping down beside her, Griff grabbed her shoulders, shaking her.

"Carrie." Eyes closed tight, she didn't budge. Touching her cheek, he cringed at the stark cold of her skin. Drawing his hand away, he shook her again. "Carrie. Wake up."

A low groan preceded her eyelids fluttering. "Come on, Carrie. Open your eyes."

She tried again, this time keeping them open to thin slits. "Griff?"

"It's me, sweetheart. I'm going to pick you up and take you inside. All right?"

Instead of answering, she burrowed deeper into the coat she wore.

Slipping his arms under her back and legs, he lifted Carrie against his chest. Moaning, she wrapped her arms around his neck.

Opening his front door, he set her on his bed, knowing the stove would heat the small room faster than the larger living room. Grabbing two blankets, he tucked them around her before closing the bedroom door and building a fire.

Taking a closer look, he saw her lips were blue, the skin around her eyes and mouth drawn tight. Picking up one of her hands, he rubbed until the skin warmed. He did the same with her other hand.

Pulling off the damp hat, he covered her hair with a towel, then did the same with her boots. Her feet were chilled clear through. Rubbing them the same as her hands, he wrapped both in a small blanket, pointing her legs toward the wood stove.

As the room heated, he boiled a pot of water on the stove, knowing Carrie preferred tea in the evening. Preparing tea, he took the cup into the bedroom, surprised to see her sitting up on the bed.

"You're awake." Setting the cup on the table next to the bed, he cupped her face with his hands. "How are you feeling?"

"I'm fine, Griff. Why are you so worried?"

Sitting next to her on the bed, his hands covered hers. "You fell asleep in the chair on my porch. When I found you, your face and hands were as cold as ice."

Brows drawing together, she stared at Griff. "I fell asleep?"

"You scared me, sweetheart. It took a while to wake you, then you fell back asleep. You were too cold to stay awake."

"So you brought me in here?"

Griff glanced around his bedroom, wincing at the austere feel of his home. "I had to warm you up fast. This seemed to be the best idea." Handing her the tea, he steadied it while she took several small sips.

"I wanted to talk with you, Griff. It had been so long, and I thought, well...I'm not certain what I thought except I missed you."

Those simple words touched a chord in his heart, as well as triggered a flash of guilt through him. He'd been hesitant to speak with Carrie, unsure how she'd see him after they'd come so close to death.

"If you're wondering, I don't blame you for what happened, Griff. Who would've been able to predict Dugan would follow us up the mountain?" Reaching out, she set her hand over his. "How were we to know the judge and Trina would follow him? You saved my life by covering me with your body. They saved our lives by killing Dugan. It all worked out as it was supposed to."

He marveled at how her uncomplicated explanation absolved him of what he'd considered his own failure. Setting her cup aside, his hand slid behind her neck as he bent closer.

"I love you, Carrie." Before she could respond, his mouth covered hers in a soft, warm kiss. Lifting his head, a slow smile spread across his face. "There's no other woman I want in my future. Marry me. Be my wife, and we'll build our future together."

Lips slightly parted, eyes moist with emotion, she pressed her lips to his. "I love you, Griff. When I dream about my future, you're the only man I see."

Stroking a hand over her hair, he kissed her forehead. "Is that a yes?"

Wrapping both arms around his neck, she pulled him down. "A million yeses, Griff. As many as you need."

Epilogue

Three weeks later…

"I now pronounce you man and wife." Reverend Paige hesitated a moment while Griff kissed his bride. Unchaste and long, the attendees in the church hooted, howled, and clapped at their friends' unapologetic performance.

Clearing his throat, the reverend continued. "May I present Mr. and Mrs. Griffin MacKenzie."

Griff broke the kiss, turning a flushed and laughing Carrie toward those who'd come to watch their wedding. Holding up their joined hands, Griff's smile matched his bride's.

Bram MacLaren and his brother, Thane, had stood up for their longtime friend, while Francesca and Rachel stood beside Carrie. The four followed the couple down the aisle, meeting up with their spouses.

All except Thane, who joined a group of single men including deputies Jonas Taylor, Tucker Nolan, and Morgan Wheeler, who'd recently returned to work after an almost life-ending bullet wound. The four men followed everyone else to the community room behind the church where the reception would be held.

Lately, Thane had made it a habit to ride into town late on Saturday afternoons to join whichever of the deputies weren't working for supper at the boardinghouse or McCall's. Sometimes, the MacLaren ranch hands, Kev and Vince Latham, would ride with him. More than once, Thane had bunked down at the house the three deputies shared next to the clinic.

Stepping inside the large room, he crossed his arms, surveying the tables laden with food and punch. A separate table held a variety of cakes, fruit breads, and candies the women had made for the wedding.

"Never thought I'd see Griff marry." Thane grinned at his friend's beaming face.

"Why's that?" Morgan followed Thane's gaze.

"Don't recall him ever courting a woman back in California. Fact is, I've never heard him talk much about women at all."

"He sure picked a good one." Jonas nodded toward another couple not far from Griff and Carrie. "Cole seems to have a strong interest in Angie Banderas's friend, Martha. She's a real nice lady, and a good cook." Cole Santori had been a deputy in Splendor about as long as Morgan, Tucker, and Jonas.

Tucker shifted toward one of Carrie's friends, who stood behind one of the food tables. "I've been thinking of courting one of the women who came west with Carrie."

Jonas lifted a brow. "Which one?"

"Don't know that it matters. Maybe Amelia Newhall."

"Pretty sure you should have a real interest in a woman before you decide to court her." Morgan grinned.

Thane listened to the easy banter of his friends, his gaze moving over the crowd. In one corner were a group of women with babies born in the last year. Abby Brandt held her daughter, Sadie, Ginny Pelletier rocked Charlotte, and Chloe Mason chattered to her mother, Lydia. The one baby boy, Grady DeBell, was being fed by his mother, Beauty.

He found himself wondering when his brother, Bram, and his wife, Selina, would be having children. The thought brought an odd yearning in an area real close to his heart. Telling himself he had plenty of time to find a woman and start a family, Thane's attention moved to Judge Hoodoo Hardin.

The judge stood with a group of men, including Enoch Weaver, a man considered by many to be the town drunk. Thane knew the truth about the keen witted man and his successful background as an attorney. Enoch and Hoodoo had become fast friends after the shootout on the mountain.

Once Hoodoo realized he wasn't going to die during his search for Dugan, he'd decided to stay in Splendor for a while. Thane had heard the two older men often sat outside the jail, debating points of law, and how they would've handled certain cases.

"Come on, MacLaren. Let's grab ourselves a couple of women and dance." Jonas grabbed his arm, heading straight toward Amelia Newhall and Rose Keenan.

Any thoughts of a future, and possible family, fled as Thane twirled Rose around the floor. Her bright smile and beautiful laughter brought an odd sense of joy to a body in need of more than hard work.

As the song ended and they continued dancing to the next one, Thane realized he had a pretty good life. Splendor had become his home. A place filled with good people who'd be there in the hard times as well as the joyous days. People who'd be his friends for life.

Enjoy the Redemption Mountain books? Here's another series you might want to read. **MacLarens of Boundary Mountain** historical western romance series.

If you want to keep current on all my preorders, new releases, and other happenings, sign up for my newsletter at http://www.shirleendavies.com/contact-me.html

A Note from Shirleen

Thank you for taking the time to read **Rocky Basin**!

If you enjoyed it, please consider telling your friends or posting a short review. Word of mouth is an author's best friend and much appreciated.

I care about quality, so if you find something in error, please contact me via email at
shirleen@shirleendavies.com

Books by Shirleen Davies

Historical Western Romance Series

Redemption Mountain

Redemption's Edge, Book One
Wildfire Creek, Book Two
Sunrise Ridge, Book Three
Dixie Moon, Book Four
Survivor Pass, Book Five
Promise Trail, Book Six
Deep River, Book Seven
Courage Canyon, Book Eight
Forsaken Falls, Book Nine
Solitude Gorge, Book Ten
Rogue Rapids, Book Eleven
Angel Peak, Book Twelve
Restless Wind, Book Thirteen
Storm Summit, Book Fourteen
Mystery Mesa, Book Fifteen
Thunder Valley, Book Sixteen
A Very Splendor Christmas, Holiday Novella, Book
Seventeen
Paradise Point, Book Eighteen,
Silent Sunset, Book Nineteen
Rocky Basin, Book Twenty
Captive Dawn, Book Twenty-One, Coming Next in the
Series!

MacLarens of Fire Mountain

Tougher than the Rest, Book One
Faster than the Rest, Book Two
Harder than the Rest, Book Three
Stronger than the Rest, Book Four
Deadlier than the Rest, Book Five
Wilder than the Rest, Book Six

MacLarens of Boundary Mountain

Colin's Quest, Book One,
Brodie's Gamble, Book Two
Quinn's Honor, Book Three
Sam's Legacy, Book Four
Heather's Choice, Book Five
Nate's Destiny, Book Six
Blaine's Wager, Book Seven
Fletcher's Pride, Book Eight
Bay's Desire, Book Nine
Cam's Hope, Book Ten

Romantic Suspense

Eternal Brethren, Military Romantic Suspense

Steadfast, Book One
Shattered, Book Two
Haunted, Book Three
Untamed, Book Four

Devoted, Book Five
Faithful, Book Six
Exposed, Book Seven
Undaunted, Book Eight
Resolute, Book Nine
Unspoken, Book Ten
Defiant, Book Eleven
Consumed, Book Twelve, Coming Next in the Series!

Peregrine Bay, Romantic Suspense

Reclaiming Love, Book One
Our Kind of Love, Book Two
Edge of Love, Book Three, Coming Next in the Series!

Contemporary Western Romance Series

MacLarens of Fire Mountain

Second Summer, Book One
Hard Landing, Book Two
One More Day, Book Three
All Your Nights, Book Four
Always Love You, Book Five
Hearts Don't Lie, Book Six
No Getting Over You, Book Seven
'Til the Sun Comes Up, Book Eight
Foolish Heart, Book Nine

Macklins of Whiskey Bend

Thorn, Book One
Del, Book Two
Boone, Book Three
Kell, Book Four, Coming Next in the Series!

Find all of my books at:
https://www.shirleendavies.com/books.html

About Shirleen

Shirleen Davies writes romance—historical, contemporary, and romantic suspense. She grew up in Southern California, attended Oregon State University, and has degrees from San Diego State University and the University of Maryland. During the day she provides consulting services to small and mid-sized businesses. But her real passion is writing emotionally charged stories of flawed people who find redemption through love and acceptance. She now lives with her husband in a beautiful town in northern Arizona.

I love to hear from my readers!

Send me an email: shirleen@shirleendavies.com
Visit my Website: https://www.shirleendavies.com/
Sign up to be notified of New Releases:
https://www.shirleendavies.com/contact/
Follow me on Amazon:
http://www.amazon.com/author/shirleendavies
Follow me on BookBub:
https://www.bookbub.com/authors/shirleen-davies

Other ways to connect with me:

Facebook Author Page:
http://www.facebook.com/shirleendaviesauthor
Twitter: www.twitter.com/shirleendavies
Pinterest: http://pinterest.com/shirleendavies

Instagram:
https://www.instagram.com/shirleendavies_author/
TikTok: https://vm.tiktok.com/ZMRMqD9a3/

Avalanche Ranch Press, LLC
PO Box 12618
Prescott, AZ 86304

Rocky Basin is a work of fiction. Names, characters, places, and incidents are either products of the author's imagination or used fictitiously. Any resemblance to actual events, locales, or persons, living or dead, is wholly coincidental.